"It's as easy as you want it to be, Laney."

Logan stood behind her, looking out over the pastures and orchards that made up the farm. All of it overgrown and snow-covered now, but he remembered the years that he and Laney had worked the fields together, given tours of the orchards, pretended that the beauty on the outside of the house matched what was inside.

He'd done it for her.

There'd been so many times when he'd thought about running, but he'd stuck it out because he couldn't imagine leaving Laney.

Now, leaving her was all he could think about.

"I'd like to borrow one of your dad's old cars. Is that okay with you?"

"Do you think any of them will be working after all this time?" She turned, her arm brushing his.

He stepped away, his pulse racing.

No way would he let himself think about what that meant.

Not when there was so much riding on his ability to walk away.

Books by Shirlee McCoy

Love Inspired Suspense

SHIRLEE McCOY

has always loved making up stories. As a child, she daydreamed elaborate tales in which she was the heroine—gutsy, strong and invincible. Though she soon grew out of her superhero fantasies, her love for storytelling never diminished. She knew early that she wanted to write inspirational fiction, and she began writing her first novel when she was a teenager. Still, it wasn't until her third son was born that she truly began pursuing her dream of being published. Three years later, she sold her first book. Now a busy mother of five, Shirlee is a homeschooling mom by day and an inspirational author by night. She and her husband and children live in the Pacific Northwest and share their house with a dog, two cats and a bird. You can visit her website, www.shirleemccoy.com, or email her at shirlee@shirleemccoy.com.

FUGITIVE

SHIRLEE
MCCOY

HARLEQUIN® LOVE INSPIRED® SUSPENSE

Recycling programs
for this product may
not exist in your area.

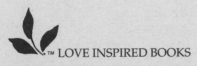 ™ LOVE INSPIRED BOOKS

ISBN-13: 978-0-373-44537-0

FUGITIVE

Copyright © 2013 by Shirlee McCoy

All rights reserved. Except for use in any review, the reproduction or utilization of this work in whole or in part in any form by any electronic, mechanical or other means, now known or hereafter invented, including xerography, photocopying and recording, or in any information storage or retrieval system, is forbidden without the written permission of the editorial office, Love Inspired Books, 233 Broadway, New York, NY 10279 U.S.A.

This is a work of fiction. Names, characters, places and incidents are either the product of the author's imagination or are used fictitiously, and any resemblance to actual persons, living or dead, business establishments, events or locales is entirely coincidental.

This edition published by arrangement with Love Inspired Books.

® and TM are trademarks of Love Inspired Books, used under license. Trademarks indicated with ® are registered in the United States Patent and Trademark Office, the Canadian Trade Marks Office and in other countries.

www.LoveInspiredBooks.com

Printed in U.S.A.

Cast your cares on the Lord and he will sustain you;
he will never let the righteous fall.
—*Psalms* 55:22

In loving memory of Joanna Trigsted. Even the shortest of lives can make an impact on the world. You are proof of that. Dance on, little one!

ONE

Just another step.

That's all he had to take.

Another step. And another.

Wind howling.

Blood dripping on fresh white snow.

Fire behind. Darkness ahead. Only one way to go. Up.

Deputy Sheriff Logan Randal pushed through winter-dry foliage, moving as quickly as his handcuffed wrists would allow. Fifteen minutes and rescue units would be at the wreck. A little longer, and the state police would know he was missing.

Missing and presumed responsible.

For the wreck.

For the officer lying dead in the culvert where Logan had dragged him before he'd realized it was too late to help. And for Officer Camden Walker, who lay bleeding beside him, unconscious and shivering beneath the jacket Logan had wrangled off Camden's deceased partner. If not for Walker, Logan would still be locked in the back of the burning police cruiser. Everything in him demanded that he go back and wait with the injured man until help arrived.

But, going back meant death. For Walker *and* for Logan.

A bullet slammed into the snow beside him, bits of earth

and ice splattering his face. He ducked behind a towering pine, then kept moving through deep forest and blowing snow, praying the gunman's aim would prove as terrible now as it had been when Logan exited the cruiser.

His foot caught on a snow-covered root, and he fell, hot white pain shooting through his head, blood still dripping from a gash on his temple. An inch closer, and the bullet that had grazed his head would have bored into his brain.

He'd be dead.

Get up. Keep moving away from the wreck. Give Walker a chance. Give yourself a chance.

The words chanted through his mind, a mantra that brought him to his feet, his orange prison jumpsuit too bright against the dark shadows of the woods and the whiteness of the snow.

Sirens screamed, the sound growing closer with every heartbeat, every breath.

Please, God, let them be close enough to chase the gunman away from Walker.

He didn't need another life on his head, didn't need someone else's blood on his hands. Didn't need anything but a chance to prove he was innocent. Not just of arranging the ambush that had freed him from prison, but of the crime a jury of eight had just convicted him of.

A half a million dollars' worth of heroin missing from the evidence room. A hundred thousand dollars in an offshore bank account in Logan's name. A paper trail of evidence that led straight to him.

Someone had worked hard to frame Logan for the crime.

Whoever it was had succeeded.

Apparently, that same person now wanted him dead.

But that wasn't going to happen. No way did Logan plan to die a felon and a murderer. No doubt that was exactly what his enemy wanted. If he was caught by the police, he'd be tried for the murder of the fallen officer. If he was caught by the men in the SUV who'd run the cruiser off the road, he'd probably be killed and left to rot where no one would ever find him.

A lose-lose situation.

He had to escape. Had to prove his innocence. Had to get back the life he'd worked so hard for.

He shoved through snow-covered foliage, ducking under pine boughs, aiming up the mountain. The wind whipped through his jumpsuit, snow blasting against his face.

Sirens pierced the air, their endless shriek joining the wild howl of the wind. A fifteen-minute head start wasn't much, but it was something, and in this weather, it might just be enough.

He struggled up the steeply inclined ridge, snow falling heavier and harder, the swirling white making him dizzy. Blood loss making him dizzier.

He looked back, saw a speck of orange fire in a gray world, flashes of red and blue reflecting on pure white ground. He was making progress, but to where? Miles of wilderness could hide him. It could also kill him.

He glanced around, searching for signs of civilization. He knew the area well, but that didn't mean he could find his way to safety. This part of eastern Washington was sparsely populated, the mountains dotted with hunting cabins. If he could find a hunting trail, make his way to a cabin, he'd live through the night. If he couldn't…

He refused the thought and kept slogging toward the top of the ridge, breath panting, body shaking with cold. The sirens faded, the wind's howl the only sound in the deepening storm.

The handcuffs weighed him down, the freezing metal only adding to the cold bite of the wind. He was shivering convulsively, and he knew what that meant. He had to get to shelter, and he had to do it fast.

His feet were frozen logs, catching on every hidden rock and jutting root. He caught himself once, twice, fell the third time, going down hard. Winded, he lay where he'd fallen, the snow more comfortable than it should have been, the cold not so cold anymore.

He forced himself up, disoriented, not sure which direction he'd been heading or where he'd come from. Trees to the left, the right, up ahead...

He squinted, sure he saw a glimmer of light through the trees, distant but beckoning.

God, please let it be more than a hallucination.

He moved toward it, the trees blocking, then revealing, then blocking his view again.

Still there.

All he had to do was keep walking.

Gusting wind rattled the cabin's windows and howled beneath its eves, the sounds shivering along Laney Jefferson's spine as she bent over the cold hearth and built a fire. Outside, fat snowflakes fell from the purple-blue sky and lay thick on the roof of the Jeep. It was stupid to have made this trip in the dead of winter, but putting it off wouldn't have made it any more appealing. Besides, Valentine's Day was just a week away, and she'd rather spend it cleaning out her parents' house than spend it alone in Seattle.

Stopping at William's cabin on the way to Green Bluff had made sense when she'd been planning the trip to her childhood home. Clean out the cabin, clean out her parents' house, clean out the cobwebs of the past that seemed to be keeping her from moving into the future. She'd been praying about the trip since she'd gotten the letter from her father's attorney saying that she'd inherited Mackey Manor and the hundred acres of farmland that went with it.

She'd wanted to turn her back on the legacy, wanted to go on pretending that her life had started the day she'd left Green Bluff and run to Seattle, but she'd had no peace about it.

She'd spent three months planning and plotting and trying to convince herself that she should return to the place she despised. Those months had made her realize just how easily she'd shoved aside her childhood and how tightly she'd been holding on to the dreams she'd built with William. Dreams that had died with him.

Move on.

That had become her mantra.

So, it *had* made perfect sense to take a two-week vacation in the middle of February, make the trip back across Washington, tying up the loose ends of her life as she went.

She wasn't sure how much sense it made now that the storm of the century was blowing through the eastern part of the state.

She shoved paper under the fire log she'd brought from home, struck a match and tossed it in. If William had been around, he'd have taken care of that. He'd also have braved the wind and snow to grab logs from the back porch. He wasn't, so Laney went herself, pulling her hood over her hair and walking out the back door. Frigid wind cut through her coat and chilled her to the bone as she lifted an armful of wood from the neat pile that William had left on the covered back porch the last time they'd been there.

Two and a half years ago.

Had it really been that long?

They'd been married less time than that. Just eighteen months, and she'd thought they would have forever. Instead, she'd been without William for longer than she'd been with him.

She walked back inside, the wind slamming the door closed behind her. She ignored it as she chose the driest log and set it on top of the burning kindling. It was easy enough to make a fire. She'd learned the skill years ago, but doing this herself, *here* where she and William had once bent close and worked together, it hurt more than she'd expected it to.

She nudged the log deeper into the fire. Sparks flew, wood crackled and something banged against the back door.

She jumped, whirling to face the door and whatever was outside it.

The wind.

It had to be.

But her racing pulse said different. So did the hair standing up on the back of her neck.

Bang!

The door shuddered, the weight of whatever was out there seeming to press in, demanding entry.

She grabbed the fireplace poker and walked to the door. "Who's there?"

No one answered.

She hadn't really expected anyone to because she couldn't imagine that anyone was wandering through the mountains during a winter storm. A tree branch must have flown into the door.

Two tree branches?

The wind was certainly blowing hard enough to tear off pieces of old pine trees, and there were plenty of those around the cabin.

She opened the door, determined to prove it to herself.

A shadow lurched through the doorway, white and gray and strangely dead looking. She screamed, and screamed again as the figure stumbled into her, knocking her to the ground.

Breathless, she twisted, fighting against deadweight and icy cold, then realizing suddenly that she was fighting herself. That her attacker was limp and heavy and motionless. She shoved him sideways and scrambled out from beneath him, her breath panting.

The poker! Where was it?

She snatched it from the ground, backing away, her heart pounding wildly in her ears.

Go! Now! Before he gets up!

She reached blindly, grabbing her purse from the hook near the front door, snatching her coat from the rocking chair and never taking her eyes off the motionless man.

The *dead* man?

Snow blew across his prone body, the back door banging against his legs and feet as the wind tried to push it shut. No response from him. Not even a twitch. Facedown, features hidden, everything about him still and silent.

She took a step closer, afraid he *was* dead.

Dark hair. Orange jumpsuit that looked crisp and frozen rather than wet. It had to be prison issue, which meant he had to be a prisoner. An escaped one. The state prison was twenty miles away. Had he walked that far?

Did it matter?

She needed to get out before he got up. Run before he recovered enough to take a hostage.

She turned her back to him, her hands shaking as she unlocked the front door. She'd head down the mountain, find a spot where she could get a cell phone signal and call the police.

"Help me."

Two words. Raw and hot and rasping.

She wanted to ignore them.

She couldn't.

She pressed her back to the door and kept her hand on the knob. "I'll call for help as soon as I get far enough down the mountain to get a signal. You'll be okay until the rescue crew gets here."

"Don't." He raised his head, his eyes midnight-blue in his

gray-white face. Dark lashes wet from melting snow. Blood seeping down his face.

His very familiar face.

"Logan?" It couldn't be.

She knelt beside him, her hand shaking as she touched his cheek and brushed hair from his forehead, looking for the thin white scar near his hairline.

There. Just like she'd known it would be.

"What happened?" she whispered.

His eyes drifted closed, and he didn't respond.

She grabbed a blanket from the trunk at the end of the bed, her throat aching with all the memories she'd shoved out of her mind and done her very best to forget.

"You have to get up. I need to close the door, and you've got to warm up." She slid her arm around his shoulders, tried to nudge him into motion. He felt different. Thirteen years had built muscle and weight on his lean frame, made the twenty-year-old kid that he'd been into a man.

A *wanted* man.

She shuddered, the cold wetness of his jumpsuit seeping into her sweater and jeans as she tried to maneuver him out of the doorway. He rolled onto his back, his hand capturing hers so unexpectedly that her heart jumped. Cuffs clanked, the frigid metal burning against her arm, Logan's grip tight and hard as he pulled her closer.

"Laney?" he rasped, his breath hot against her cheek.

"Yes."

"Go."

"What?"

"Leave. *Now.*" He released his hold, grabbed the edges of the blanket with dead-white hands and turned onto his side, closing her out in a way he'd never done when she'd been a little girl desperate for someone to believe in.

"Your hands may be frostbitten. We need to get—"

He snatched her wrist and yanked her so close she could see every fleck of silver in his eyes. He had blood on his cheek, frozen against his grayish skin, and blood on the front of his jumpsuit. "*We* don't need to do anything. *You* need to go."

His words were slurred, his body stiff as he released his grip and struggled to his feet.

She didn't touch him this time. Didn't try to help as he shuffled to the fireplace and dropped down in front of it.

Thirteen years was a long time.

He could have become anyone or anything in those years.

But she still couldn't leave him.

She owed him too much.

She set the teakettle on the propane stove and took coffee from the box of supplies she'd left on the table.

"Did you hear me? I want you to leave," he said, his back to Laney, the blanket shrouding his head and covering his shoulders. Melted snow pooled around him, tinged pink with blood.

"You're bleeding."

"Not your problem." He didn't move, didn't glance her way.

"There's a first aid kit in my Jeep. I'll—"

"You don't seem to get it, Laney. Being around me is dangerous. You need to leave while you still can."

She took another blanket from the chest and threw it over his shoulders. "Here. Coffee will be ready in a minute."

Suddenly, he was up, looming over her. Cold, cold expression and fiery eyes, a stranger lurking behind an old friend's face. She shivered and tried to step back, but he held her in place with his eyes and the sheer force of his will.

"I'm a felon, Laney. Tried and convicted. You want to spend the night in this cabin with me? You want to risk that?"

"I—"

"Drive off this mountain and forget you ever saw me." He dropped back down in front of the fire, shivering beneath the blanket. Closed in and closed up and absolutely committed to chasing Laney away.

The small part of her, the remnant of the scared kid she'd been when she'd run from Green Bluff, wanted to give him what he wanted. The other part, the bigger part, refused to. He'd helped her all those years ago. If not for Logan, she'd never have gotten her college degree, become an interior designer, met William and married him. Without Logan, the Laney she was now wouldn't exist.

She took the keys from her purse and stepped out into the blowing snow, heading for the Jeep and the first aid kit she kept there. No matter what Logan had become, no matter who, she'd make sure he was warm and dry and safe because, once upon a time, he'd done exactly the same for her.

TWO

Cold.

Hot.

Logan wasn't sure which he was, but he was shaking violently, his teeth knocking together.

He shouldn't have sent Laney away. She had a Jeep, a way off the mountain. All he had were frozen fingers and leaden feet, but he couldn't pull her into his troubles. Couldn't risk her life in an effort to save his own.

Laney. Grown up and confident, her soft green eyes looking straight into his. It had been thirteen years since he'd handed her two thousand dollars and a bus ticket to Seattle, but he'd have known her anywhere. Her pretty face and solemn eyes. Her white-blond hair that had only darkened a little as she'd grown older. He'd seen her in the window of her parents' oversize home the day that he'd arrived at Mildred and Josiah Mackey's place. He'd been nearly fifteen and in so much trouble that a farmhouse in the middle of nowhere was the only place that would have him. He hadn't been interested in the tiny little blonde with her perfect hair and perfect life. Until he'd realized that nothing about Laney's life was perfect. Then, he'd wanted nothing more than to free her from the prison in which she lived.

He wrapped the blanket tightly around his shoulders, the

memories more vivid than they should have been. Hypothermia?

Probably.

He'd warm up, though. Find some way to rid himself of the cuffs. He wasn't foolish enough to think he had unlimited time. The police were already on the hunt. So were the men who'd run the cruiser off the road. He had to warm up quickly and get moving again. And come up with a plan to prove his innocence.

He grabbed a mug from a cupboard and poured hot water from the whistling teakettle into it, his hands burning as he wrapped them around the ceramic.

"Logan?" Laney's voice came from far away, and he realized he'd closed his eyes and was leaning against the counter, the mug still cradled in his hands. He blinked, trying to bring her into focus.

No perfect hair now.

Curls escaped her long braid, falling against smooth, pale cheeks. She looked scared. She should be.

He straightened, setting the cup on the counter. "I told you to leave."

"You have a pretty deep cut. You're going to need stitches." She ignored the comment and dabbed his temple with an alcohol-soaked cotton ball.

He smelled the fumes but felt nothing.

Not a good sign.

"What do you suggest? A trip to the nearest hospital?" He motioned toward his prison uniform, the cuffs on his wrists clanking.

"I see you haven't outgrown your sarcasm." She dabbed at the cut again, swiping a fresh cotton ball down his cheek.

"I'm afraid your parents were never quite able to beat it out of me," he responded and regretted it immediately. He *had* outgrown sarcasm and his need for revenge. He had become what he'd always wanted to be, part of a community that he had loved, doing a job that he'd loved. Even, for a while, married to a woman that he'd loved.

An image of Amanda flashed through his mind.

Broken glass and her broken body and his own helplessness.

He pushed the memory away.

"I should be able to butterfly the wound closed, but you're probably going to have a scar." Laney rifled through a large first aid kit, her fingers long and delicate, the knuckles of her right hand scarred.

It would be so easy for those hands to break, so easy for the light in her eyes to be snuffed out.

"Laney, I want you to leave." He bit the words out, forcing himself to move away. The cuffs on his wrists felt heavy and cold. His body also felt heavy and cold, but he had to get her out of his life.

"I can't."

"You don't have a choice."

"Weren't you the one who once told me I had a million choices?" She pulled butterfly bandages from the kit. "Sit down so I can do this."

"I could be a murderer. A serial killer planning to make you my next victim," he spit out because it was all he had left, his last push to get her out of the cabin and to safety.

"In your current condition, I doubt you could make an ant your next victim." She pressed the bandage to his temple, her eyes cool and calm, her hand shaking.

She didn't know that he'd been a deputy sheriff for five years and had worked on the Green Bluff police force for five years before that. Didn't know that he had been falsely accused and convicted of drug trafficking.

What she didn't know, he could use against her.

For her?

It didn't matter.

All that mattered was keeping her safe.

He'd failed Amanda. And she'd died because of it.

He wouldn't fail Laney.

He yanked her hand down, then moved so close he could smell melting snow mixed with flowers in her hair. "Don't make the mistake of believing that, Laney."

"I don't believe you're a murderer. I don't believe you'd hurt me."

"Then believe you're in trouble if you're caught with me."

"Caught by the police?" Her gaze dropped to his jumpsuit.

"It's not just the police I'm worried about."

"Then who?"

"It's a long story." Too long to tell when danger was breathing down both their necks. Logan felt the clock ticking, trouble drawing near.

"We have time. The storm won't break for hours."

"How far are we from the main road?"

"Five miles." She repacked the first aid kit, putting everything back exactly where it belonged. Neat and tidy. Just the way her parents had trained her to be. He'd hated that about her when they'd met. Her perfection against his rough edges. Her pristine dresses against his worn and dirty clothes.

Now, she wore faded jeans and a soft sweater, the fabric hugging her slender curves.

"Are there other cabins nearby?"

"No. My husband bought a hundred and fifty acres from a logging company fifteen years ago. This is the only place around."

Not what he'd wanted to hear.

If this really *was* the only place around, anyone hunting him would know exactly where to look. He needed to get the cuffs off his wrists, get out of his prison orange and put on a few layers of clothing. Then, he needed to get going while he still could.

"Does your husband keep clothes up here? I'm not exactly dressed for the weather. I can pay him for everything I borrow."

"My husband passed away two years ago."

"I'm sorry."

"Me, too." She opened a trunk at the end of a queen-size bed and pulled out a pile of clothes. "You can use whatever you need."

"Thanks. Now, I just need to find a way to put them on." He lifted his cuffed wrists.

"We might be able to pick the lock." She leaned over the cuffs, her hands on his wrists as she studied the lock. Warm fingers on cold flesh. Flowers and slow waltzes in the moonlight. It had been a long time since he'd thought of any of those things. In the three years since Amanda's death, he'd mostly stayed out of the dating game. A few dinners set up by friends. A lunch here or there. Nothing that had stuck because he hadn't wanted anything to.

He stepped back, pulling his wrists from Laney's hands.

"Do you have a tool chest in your car?"

"A small one, but I doubt there's anything in there that'll take these off. I think I'll have better luck in the shop. William kept tons of tools in it." She shrugged into her coat, dragging her braid over the collar.

"Where's the shop?"

"Out back. I'll just be a minute." She opened the back door and frigid wind blew in, spraying snow across the wood floor and plastering the wet jumpsuit to Logan's frozen skin. He pulled the blankets closer, gritting his teeth. The last thing he wanted was to walk out that door and follow Laney into the cold, but he couldn't stay in the cabin while she went herself.

He walked onto the back porch, the wind biting into his

throbbing, thawing flesh. He would be frozen again before they were done, but if he was able to ditch the cuffs and the jumpsuit, it would be worth it.

"You should stay in the cabin," Laney said as she picked her way down snow-covered stairs.

"I don't think so."

"You're nearly thawed, Logan. Do you really want to freeze again?"

No.

But he didn't want her out in the storm by herself either. He didn't trust that the men who'd shot at him had run when the police showed up. Hidden? Yes. Disappeared from the picture? No way. No one went to as much trouble as they had to fail, and Logan had a feeling that the only way for them to succeed was for him to be dead, his body buried somewhere in the wilderness.

He followed Laney across the clearing. If a shop existed, it was well hidden by the night and by the storm. Snow blew into Logan's eyes, the raging wind snatching every breath before it formed. He glanced back and saw the vague outline of the cabin and light spilling out from its windows. How far would they have to go before they lost sight of both? In a storm like this, not far.

"This isn't a good idea, Laney." He snagged her coat, nearly bumping into her back when she stopped. "If we go much farther, we may not be able to find our way back."

"We're already here. William kept the workshop locked, but there's a spare key." She brushed snow from a birdhouse nailed to the side of a large building, her fingers sliding under it. It seemed to take forever, but she finally pulled out a key.

Logan crowded into the shop behind her, catching a whiff of wood chips and sawdust and summer flowers.

"There's a light here somewhere." Fabric rustled as Laney moved, and a light went on, spilling into the cavernous room.

She hadn't been exaggerating when she'd said her husband had tools. Logan figured there were a couple of tons of tools in the building. Table saws. Band saws. Lathes. A plainer. Rows of shelves that housed chisels and sanders. Handsaws hung from the far wall. Antique and new, side by side. Everything orderly and neat.

Obviously, William had loved his tools.

"I think we can drill through the lock mechanism to open the cuffs," Laney said, her voice tight and her movements stiff as she walked to one of the shelves and lifted an electric drill. Was it the shop or the situation that had her tense?

"You don't have to help me, Laney. It would be better if you didn't," he said gently because he wanted her to take the out he was offering, to run before anyone knew that they'd ever been together.

"You never told me why." She grabbed a drill from a tool chest, patted a worktable. "Put your hands here."

"Why what?" he asked, placing his hands palm down on smooth wood.

"Why it's so dangerous for us to be together. Why you think someone other than the police is after you." She aimed the drill straight into the cuff lock, her hands steady. If she was nervous, it didn't show, and he couldn't help thinking how different she was from the scared and anxious girl he used to know.

"The police cruiser that was taking me to state prison was run off the road. The driver was shot and killed. Another officer was wounded. Whoever was responsible took a shot at me."

"Why would someone help you escape and then kill you?"

"That's a good question, and I don't have an answer." But he would. All he needed was time and a place to hunker down and plan.

"Why were you on your way to state prison?" The drill whined and protested, a few sparks flying as she pressed down.

"I was convicted of trafficking in illegal narcotics."

"Were you guilty?" Laney asked—because she had to know and because she couldn't believe that the teenager who had been so adamantly opposed to drugs had turned into a man who sold them.

"No." Logan's answer was short, his hands pressed hard to the table that William had fashioned out of thick oak slabs. Laney had been there with him the weekend he'd finished it. She had smiled as he'd caressed the golden wood and imagined out loud all of the things he could create on it.

The thought of selling his cabin and shop and everything in them made her stomach churn.

Her hand slipped, the drill sliding from the lock and digging into the wood.

"Careful." Logan grabbed her hand, holding it steady for a moment.

"Sorry." She pressed the drill in again and focused her attention on forcing the lock open. It took three tries, but the lock finally popped. Not a pretty job, but done. "You're free."

"Thanks." Logan slid out of the cuffs, rubbing the raw red welts on his wrists. He was still shivering, but he had some color in his face.

Good.

Not so good that she'd just freed a convict from handcuffs. *She* might believe Logan's story, but a jury hadn't.

"We should go back to the cabin." She put the drill back exactly where William had always kept it, then ran her finger over the ding it had made in the table.

For some reason, tears burned behind her eyes.

Not grief. She'd cried a million tears in the weeks after William died. Maybe it was just sadness over all the dreams she'd never live with him.

"You okay?" Logan lifted her hand from the wood and ran his thumb across her knuckles. Even hurt and cold, he seemed larger than life, his dark blue gaze so intense that she had to look away.

"Fine. I just think we should get back and start planning how we're going to get off the mountain."

"*We're* not going to get me off. *I'm* going to do it. You're going to pretend that you never saw me." He tugged her outside and back into the cabin, slamming the door against the bitter cold. The fire had nearly died, and Laney shrugged out of her coat, shivering a little as she piled logs on the embers and stoked them to life.

Logan didn't speak as he grabbed the pile of clothes she'd pulled out for him. He didn't say a word as he walked into the small bathroom and closed the door.

She wondered if he'd return, or if he'd climb out the bathroom window and disappear into the storm.

Would she go after him if he did?

She'd been raised to follow the rules, to strive for perfection. Nothing short of that had ever been acceptable. As an adult, she'd tried to move past the need for flawless living. She'd tried to concentrate on what God wanted from her rather than what people wanted. She'd let her hair be messy sometimes, allowed herself to dress in jeans and sweaters.

Still, she'd never skirted the law, and in helping Logan she'd done more than that. She'd broken it.

The bathroom door opened, and he walked out, William's flannel shirt hanging open over a black T-shirt. His faded jeans hung low on Logan's leaner hips. William had been shorter, a little broader and a lot older. On him, the clothes had looked comfortable and easy.

On Logan...

She frowned, pouring still-warm water into a mug. "Warmer?"

"Much. And, now that I am, I really need you to leave. If this is the only cabin on the mountain—"

"It is."

"Then eventually someone is going to show up here looking for me. I don't want you here when it happens."

"If I leave, how will *you* get off the mountain?"

"I'll manage."

"You can't walk out. It's too far."

"Like I said, I'll manage. Did your husband keep a handgun around?"

"In the lockbox on the top shelf of the closet," she responded and then wished she hadn't. She'd already broken the law. She was breaking it again by providing a felon with a firearm.

He grabbed the box and set it on the satiny wood of the little table William had crafted on their last visit to the cabin together.

"Do you know the combination?"

"Why do you need a gun?" she asked, unable to look away as Logan fiddled with the combination lock. With his dark hair almost dry and his chin shadowed with the beginning of a beard, he looked tough and dangerous.

"I'm not planning to kill a cop with it, if that's what you're thinking."

"I'm *thinking* that helping you get out of those cuffs was one thing. Giving you a weapon is something else. Unless you have a really good reason for wanting it, it's probably better that it stays locked up."

"It's not a weapon—it's a firearm. And I'm only planning to use it for protection." He looked up from the box, his eyes blazing. Familiar eyes, and she couldn't deny them, couldn't turn away from the truth she saw there. She rattled off the combination, and he lifted the pistol, checking to see if it was loaded and then grabbing the ammunition that William had locked up with it.

"I'd better go," she said because looking at him wearing William's clothes and carrying William's firearm made her chest tight and her stomach ache. She'd loved William. He'd been her best friend and confidant. Her cheerleader and supporter. With him, she'd had freedom from the chaos and drama that she'd grown up with.

The thing was, she'd loved Logan, too, all those years ago. Had loved him with the kind of love only a child who'd been desperate for affection could feel.

She didn't want to leave him, but she didn't know how she could stay when staying meant turmoil and trouble. She'd run from that thirteen years ago. And she'd lived more than a decade with peace and stability and order in her life.

"Be careful on the roads, and don't stop for anything but a marked police cruiser," Logan said as she opened the front door.

She nodded but couldn't speak. Her eyes burned with tears, all the things Logan had done for her when she was young and hurting and scared crowding into her brain.

Don't cry, Laney. Don't give them that power over you.

Those were the first words he'd ever spoken to her. She'd shoved the memory so far back in her mind, she hadn't known it was still there.

She walked outside, let the wind cool her hot face and burning eyes and tried to tell herself that she wasn't abandoning the man who'd lived in her parents' home for five years because he hadn't wanted to abandon her.

She was doing the right thing. She had to believe that, had to trust that God's plan would work itself out. *He* would protect Logan.

He didn't need Laney's help for that.

Still…

Thirteen years, and Logan was suddenly back in her life.
That had to mean something.

Didn't it?

She slid behind the wheel of the Jeep, her gaze jumping to
the cabin. She needed to drive away, but she couldn't quite
make herself start the engine.

The cabin door opened, and Logan appeared, silhouetted in
the light. He walked to the car, his stride long and confident.

She unrolled the window as he approached.

"Did you change your mind about wanting a ride?" she
asked, half hoping that he'd say he had. Half hoping that he
wouldn't.

"I need to toss this into the woods. Ten minutes, and it'll
be covered with snow." He held up his prison uniform. "If
anyone finds it, they'll assume I'm hypothermic and out of
my mind with it. I don't want anyone knowing I was here.
Not for a while, anyway."

"Logan…"

She wasn't sure what she planned to say, what she *should*
say.

"Everything is going to be okay," he cut in before she could
gather her thoughts. "Now, go. Because the longer you sit
there, the longer I'm going to be standing out here, and the
colder we're both going to get."

He meant it.

She was absolutely sure that he'd stand there until she left.
She nodded, rolled up the window and started the engine,
her heart beating a heavy, hard rhythm as she pulled away.

THREE

Snow splattered against the Jeep's windshield and Laney turned on the wipers, her hand shaking a little.

She had to do this.

Had to.

Because it was what Logan wanted, and because Laney's trip back home was designed to help her close the door to the past. Not revisit it.

She frowned, her hands tight on the steering wheel, snow swirling as she inched down the long driveway. She'd given herself two weeks to clean out the cabin and her parents' house. Two weeks to get them both on the market and return to her interior design job and to her clients.

She hadn't expected it to be easy, but she *had* expected it to go smoothly. She'd planned everything out—called the lawyer who'd handled her father's estate after he'd died and asked him to have the electricity turned back on at the farmhouse, contacted a real estate agent and a contractor, asked friends to water her plants while she was gone.

Yeah, she'd planned everything out, but she hadn't planned on Logan.

Hadn't planned on having to turn her back on a part of the past that was suddenly very much in the present.

She flipped on the heat, trying to drive away the chill in her bones.

A light flashed somewhere below. It was just a glimmer that she wasn't even sure she'd seen, but her pulse jumped, adrenaline streaming through her blood.

Just keep going, keep driving.

She wanted to, but her foot had a mind of its own, pressing on the brake so that the Jeep eased to a stop.

She sat for a moment, peering into the storm, her body tense as she waited for some sign that there really was someone else on the mountain.

There! Another glimmer of light.

The police?

Someone worse?

She thought about Logan, completely unaware of the threat closing in on him.

Just. Keep. Going.

But she couldn't.

He'd done too much for her all those years ago, and she couldn't leave without warning him.

She put her car in reverse and backed toward the cabin, her heart racing with fear. Logan had warned her that trouble was coming. He'd told her to leave. Alone, though, trapped on the mountain with no transportation, he'd die.

She couldn't let that happen.

No matter how terrified she was.

Danger.

Logan could feel it coming as he put on a coat that he'd found in the closet and shoved his feet into hiking boots that were a size too small. He tucked the gun into one pocket of the coat and extra ammo into the other, then searched the drawers and cupboards in the kitchen, grabbing matches and a slender paring knife. He shoved the first into his back pocket and tucked the other into his boot. This wasn't his way, digging through other people's things and searching for whatever he could put to use. He felt like the criminal the jury had said he was.

He doused the fire and turned off the lights.

He stood in the pitch blackness of the cabin and prayed that God would lead him down the mountain and to safety.

Headlights splashed across the front windows, and he knew that he needed to run. He *wanted* to run, but he felt weak, shaky, still disoriented, his body trying to thaw but still so cold that his teeth chattered.

Going outside to toss the jumpsuit had been risky, but he'd had to do it. For Laney's sake. Maybe even for his own. He didn't want there to be any link between the two of them.

He walked to the back door, his legs heavy, his mind sluggish. Another hour in the cold would probably kill him. He knew it, but he didn't have much of a choice. Die trying to live, or give up and just die?

Footsteps pounded on the front porch, and he pulled the gun, waited as the doorknob turned and aimed as the door flew open.

Someone raced into the cabin, whirled in the darkness, hair swinging in a long pale rope.

"Logan?" Laney called, her slender figure silhouetted against the gray night revealed by the open door.

"Do you know how close you just came to dying?" Logan growled, his legs weak from what had almost happened. If he hadn't served as a police officer for a decade, he might have pulled the trigger before he realized who was on the other end of the barrel.

"You can lecture me later. I saw lights down the mountain. We have to get out of here." She grabbed his hand and yanked him out into the storm.

He let her because sending her alone toward whatever

was coming up the mountain felt like sending a lamb into a lion's den.

"Are you sure you saw lights?"

"Yes. I'm not sure if they were on the road or in the woods, but they shouldn't have been there. There's nothing between here and the highway but trees." She opened the door of her Jeep, motioned for him to climb in then ran to the driver's side and slid behind the wheel. "Should I head down or up? The road goes both ways."

"How far up are we talking? Can we get to the other side of the mountain or will we hit a dead end somewhere?"

"I don't know. William and I never walked to the end of the road. The farthest we ever went was a couple of miles."

"I think we'd better try it. Worst-case scenario, we'll get out and walk down the other side of the mountain."

He hoped it wouldn't come to that, but he'd rather ride away from certain danger than into it.

"Okay." Laney pulled away from the cabin, the Jeep crawling along the driveway, the headlights off. Snow lightened the road they turned onto, swirling down into a valley far below. The wind had died, and the trees were still and quiet. Nothing but the snow moved, and that made Logan nervous. The Jeep shimmying from side to side as Laney inched up the road made him nervous, too. If they tumbled off the side of the mountain, they wouldn't have to worry about running out of road or running into trouble.

He shifted in his seat, searching the area behind them, probing the woods. A light pierced the darkness, too bright to be a flashlight, too still to be headlights. The cabin? Another light appeared. Windows illuminating the darkness. His heart jerked.

"Think we can go any faster?" he asked, and Laney tensed.

"What's wrong?" Her voice was tight, her grip white-knuckled on the steering wheel.

"It looks like there's someone at the cabin."

"The police?"

"No." There'd be flashing emergency lights, more motion and action.

"How much of a head start do you think we have?"

"If they're on foot, plenty."

"What if they're not?"

"How about we just keep moving forward?"

"Funny. That's why I came to the cabin this weekend. To move forward," she said quietly, her voice shaking.

"Yeah?" He wanted to keep her focused on the conversation rather than her fear and the threat that was following them.

"My father left me the family property when he died. I'm supposed to be in Green Bluff tomorrow night so that I can clean out the house and get it ready to go on the market."

"You're selling your parents' place?" The property had been sitting vacant for twelve years. Logan had driven past it several times a week when he was on the force. Every time, he'd thanked God that the Mackeys had gotten what they'd deserved and that Laney hadn't had to suffer for their crimes.

"Like I said, I'm trying to move forward. Strange how I finally made the decision to let go of the past and one of the biggest parts of it is suddenly in my life again." She laughed a little, but there was more sadness than humor in the sound.

"I'm sorry, Laney."

"For what?"

"Coming back into your life."

"It's not like you planned it, Logan. It happened the same way as the first time you did. God worked it out. Who are either of us to say that it's not for the best?"

She had a point, but that didn't change the fact that Logan had endangered her or that every minute that they were together the danger grew.

They rounded a sharp curve, the car fishtailing and sliding toward the two-hundred-foot drop to their right. Laney wrangled the vehicle back into the middle of the road, her breath coming in short quick gasps.

"You doing okay?" he asked.

"This is crazy, Logan. We could be navigating switchbacks for hours, and in this kind of weather, it's just not safe."

"Want me to drive?" He'd driven in worse conditions, and he wasn't as nervous as she seemed to be. At this point, that could only play in their favor.

"Yes." The Jeep rolled to a stop, trees pressing in on one side, a gray expanse of nothing to the other, the road barely visible ahead.

"Hold on." Logan grabbed Laney's wrist before she could open the door. Her pulse throbbed rapidly beneath her skin, but her face was cool and composed.

"What?"

"I'll come around. You can just slide over. No sense in both of us going out in the cold again." He didn't give her time to argue, just got out of the Jeep.

Snow crunched beneath Logan's feet as he rounded the car, the scent of pine and the crisp winter air reminding him of home. It had been eight months since he'd been back there. Eight months since he'd hiked the bluff behind his house and inhaled the cold clean air.

He wanted to go home. He wanted it so badly, he could taste it. Every cell in his body yearned for it. Home was all he'd ever dreamed of when he was a kid. He hadn't wanted fancy clothes or toys or things. He'd just wanted that safe landing place, that soft spot where nothing mattered but just *being*.

He slid behind the wheel, taking one last deep lungful of air and catching a faint whiff of something sharp and bitter.

Fire!

He was back outside almost before the thought could register, scanning the forest below, searching for a spot of color, a plume of smoke, something to prove what his gut was saying.

"Logan? What's wrong?" Laney appeared at his elbow.

"Maybe nothing." But in the distance a black cloud billowed up toward the blue-gray sky.

"It's the cabin, isn't it?"

"I don't know."

"What else could it be?" she asked, but he didn't think she expected an answer.

"We'd better get moving." He took her arm, leading her back to the Jeep and helping her inside.

She went without protest, pulling her knees to her chest and resting her chin against them. He wanted to take her back down the mountain before she got dragged any deeper into his troubles, but the fire would bring more emergency crews, more police presence, more of everything that Logan needed to avoid. If he turned around now, he and Laney would both be arrested.

Or worse.

Anyone could be waiting on the road behind them.

Hunted, herded toward something—that's how Logan felt.

"I can still smell the fire," Laney said as she shifted in her seat and looked out the back window. All Logan could smell was the subtle scent of flowers that floated in the air every time she moved.

"It may not be as bad as we think." But Logan thought it might be worse. Someone had known that he'd been there. That same someone had set the fire. To keep him from returning to the cabin? To flush him out of hiding?

"How can it not be? It will take time for the fire crew to get to the cabin in this snow. By the time they do, all William's hard work will be gone. He built the cabin two years before we got married. He did most of the work there himself. He loved that place." The wistfulness in her words made Logan want to squeeze her hand, tell her again how sorry he was that he'd come back into her life.

"Did *you* love it?"

"I loved how happy he was when he was there. He always said he did his best work when he was in the middle of nowhere surrounded by God's creation."

"What kind of work did he do?"

"He refinished woodwork in old homes and built custom cabinets. He carved some really beautiful wood sculptures that he sold in art galleries in Seattle and San Diego."

"That explains the shop then."

"Yes. I wonder if they'll burn that, too."

"There was only one smoke plume."

"That's something." But it didn't seem like enough. Not to Laney. Not yet. She rubbed her arms, trying to chase away the chill that flowed through her blood.

"How long were you and William married?" Logan asked, and she knew he was trying to distract her, get her mind off the burning cabin. She let him because thinking about all of William's hard work burning to ashes made her eyes ache with tears she didn't want to let fall.

"Just eighteen months. We were friends for three years before that."

"Friends?" He kept his eyes on the road, but she could feel the weight of his judgment. As if being friends wasn't enough to build a marriage on. That had been what her closest friends had told her. That building a life on liking someone wasn't the same as building it on love.

"I *loved* William," she said a little too sharply.

"I wasn't questioning that."

"Then what *were* you questioning?"

"Usually people say they were dating for a certain amount of time before they were married. Not that they were friends."

"We dated for six months. That was enough." She pressed her lips together, stopping more words from flowing. She didn't need to defend her relationship with William. Didn't need to explain it. She didn't even think Logan was asking her to. Somehow, though, in the darkest part of her mind and in her deepest moments of sadness over William's death, she'd always wondered if loving him more would have saved him.

"I can understand that. I dated my wife for two years. We married the day after we graduated from college. People we knew said we were crazy, but...we just knew it was right."

"This must be hard on her. She'll be frantic when she hears that you're missing somewhere in the mountains in the middle of a snowstorm."

"Amanda died three years ago."

"I'm sorry." Such a lame thing to say, the words so powerless and futile.

"Me, too."

"Did she—"

"This might be the end of the road." Logan cut her off, the car easing to a stop a few inches from a fallen tree. "Let me see if it can be moved."

"I'll help."

"Wait until I figure out how big the tree is." He jumped out, the engine still humming, the harsh scent of smoke filling the vehicle. Laney wrinkled her nose, trying not to think of the cabin burning but unable to think of anything else. All William's hard work—the floors, the table, the cabinets—all of it gone.

She blinked back hot tears and got out of the car. It was silly to cry about *things*. They could be replaced. Besides, she hadn't planned to keep the cabin. She'd planned to sell it, and she could still sell the land it sat on.

If they ever got off of the mountain.

She grabbed hold of the small pine tree that Logan was

tugging toward the side of the road, her arm brushing his as they moved it out of the way. The air was tinged with smoke, the scent of it stinging her nose and eyes. She knew she shouldn't look down the mountain, but she looked anyway, searching until she found the dark plume of smoke she'd seen earlier. This time she could see a splash of gold in the gray-black world.

Would there be anything left when the fire crews finally got the fire under control?

"You okay?" Logan slid an arm round her waist and pulled her close. He felt warm and solid, and she thought about the years when he'd been the only person she could count on, the only one who knew the truth about her life and her parents. She'd trusted him then, but she knew little about him now. Not where he'd lived before he went to prison, not who his wife had been or how she'd died. Not whether he had children, a career, the kind of life he'd spoken about when he was a troubled teenager with big dreams.

"I will be." She turned her back on the burning cabin and the woods and got in the Jeep. She'd come here to say goodbye. This was as good a time as any to do it.

Goodbye to the past.

Hello to the future.

A fresh start. A clean break.

It's what she'd been craving for months, but running toward it was so much more difficult than she'd thought it would be. Seeing the cabin burn was such an achingly painful thing that she wondered if she were really ready to move on.

Logan slid behind the steering wheel and offered a half smile that flashed the dimple in his right cheek, and Laney's heart stirred, her mind yearning for the thing they'd had when they were kids. That solid connection, that deep knowledge of one another.

She turned away, staring out into the blowing snow as

they started back up the mountain. The landscape hushed and still, the sky gray and heavy, they could have been anywhere, heading toward anything, but they were here, on William's mountain, running for their lives together.

It was better than running alone.

She clung to that thought as they crested one final rise and then slowly made their way down the mountain toward the valley below.

FOUR

He had to get Laney to safety and leave her there before anyone knew that they'd been together. The pain in Logan's head, the foggy shivery feel of warmth seeping back into his frozen body, even the risk to his life...none of it mattered as much as that.

Laney shifted in the seat, looking over her shoulder and back the way they'd come. He doubted there was much to see. Just the falling snow, the blue-black darkness and the billowing grayish smoke from the fire. They were almost down the mountain, and he could still see it, spreading across the night sky, relentless and unchanged.

Was the fire crew there? Were the police? Had anyone put his name together with Laney's yet? It would happen. It was just a matter of time. When that happened, Laney would become a suspect, part of whatever plot the police thought Logan had hatched to stage his escape.

He couldn't let that happen to her.

"How many people knew that you were on your way to Green Bluff, Laney?" he asked. The more people who knew her plans, the more likely the police could trace her movements. That could play to her advantage, or it could be the thing that brought her down.

"My clients. My coworkers. My friends. My neighbor, Mrs. Lawrence. She's going to water my plants while I'm away."

"Do they all know that you planned to stop at the cabin?"

"My close friends do. Mrs. Lawrence does. I left a detailed itinerary so that she'd know where to reach me if there were any problems at the house."

So typical of the Laney he'd once known.

Making sure everything was perfectly in order.

"Call her and tell her that you're on your way home."

"What?"

"Tell her that the storm is too bad to continue. The pass is closed and you're staying in a hotel until the roads are clear. Once they do, you're going to return home."

"But—"

"Make the call." He tightened his grip on the steering wheel as the road widened in front of them. If the police were waiting at the entrance to the highway, no phone call would save her.

"And then what? You actually want me to go back home?"

"Yes."

"Only if you go with me."

"That will be the first place the police look once they realize that the cabin in the woods belonged to your husband and once they realize that you're Elaine Mackey."

"No one calls me Elaine. I changed my name legally when I turned eighteen. It's Laney now. Laney Jefferson since I got married."

"And you don't think that the police will be able to figure that out?"

"So what if they do? You and I knew each other a long time ago, Logan. The only people who will even remember that are in Green Bluff, and I'm sure they haven't thought about my family or you in years."

He laughed at the absurdity of anyone in Green Bluff forgetting anything that had to do with the Mackeys or him. People in the small town had long memories.

"What?"

"No one in Green Bluff has forgotten you or your parents. No one has forgotten me either."

"It's been—"

"Eight months since I was arrested for stealing heroin from the evidence locker at work and selling it for a few million dollars and about five hours since I was sentenced to prison. I was the deputy sheriff of Green Bluff before that. I'm pretty sure that no one has forgotten me."

"You never left?" She sounded surprised and a little appalled. She'd hated her life in Green Bluff. Hated the act that she'd put on for the people of the community. The only daughter of the founding father's great-great grandson, and she'd had to be perfect, pretend that her family was perfect and hide the bruises and the pain. He'd watched her do it from the time she was eleven until he'd helped her escape. He understood why she'd seen nothing good in the community, but he'd found a home there, a place where he could be more than the child of a gang leader and a prostitute. More than a foster kid shuffled from home to home, trouble to trouble. He'd found roots in Green Bluff, and he'd made sure that they were planted deep.

"I didn't see any reason to leave." Even after he'd gathered enough evidence to have Laney's parents thrown in jail for fraud, child abuse and neglect and to have her father arrested for and convicted of the murder of a fifteen-year-old foster child who had died and been buried on the Mackey property a few months before Logan arrived, Logan had known that Green Bluff would always be home.

"I guess I just figured that you'd moved away, maybe gone back to Los Angeles."

"I spent fourteen years of my life in L.A., Laney, but that

doesn't mean there was anything there for me. Call your neighbor. Tell her exactly what we discussed, okay?"

"Fine." She pulled out her cell phone and made the call, her voice cheerful and bright as she explained the change of plans. All those years of hiding the truth was paying off in a big way, but she didn't seem happy as she hung up the phone.

"Good job."

"I don't like lying to someone I care about."

"It's not a lie if you follow through. Stay in a hotel tonight. Go back home tomorrow. You can fly to Green Bluff in a week or two."

"I only have two weeks to clean out the house and get it on the market, then I have to go back to work. Besides, I told my father's lawyer that I'd be there. He's expecting me."

"Will any of that matter if you get thrown in jail?" Up ahead, the road dumped out onto the highway. No flashing lights or police blockade.

"No, but…"

"What?"

"I wanted to get it over with. Going back there, seeing the place that I hated as a kid, it doesn't fill me with warm fuzzy feelings."

"Jail won't fill you with them either."

"I get the point, Logan. You don't have to keep stressing it." Laney leaned her head against the window, trying to ease the headache building behind her eyes. She hadn't slept well the past few nights, lying awake into the early morning, telling herself that she could and would clean out her parents' house.

Such a good plan.

Completely fallen apart now.

Maybe she could hire someone to clean it out, and she could supervise things from Seattle. That's what she'd intended to do, but her father's attorney had made it clear that he thought she should handle the job. Her legacy, he'd called it, and she couldn't deny it. The Mackey house and the property it sat on had been in the family for more than a hundred years.

She'd be the last generation to have lived there.

She probably should feel better about it than she did.

"There's a sign for food and lodging. We'll pull off here and find a hotel. You can get a room for the night and go home in the morning."

"Where will you be?"

"I'll find a place."

"I can book you a room, too."

"How will you explain that to the police when they question you and the person who checked us both in?"

"I can check in and—"

"I don't want you to worry about me, Laney. Okay? I can take care of myself. I've been doing it for a long time."

A lot longer than most people. He didn't say that, but Laney knew the truth. He'd entered foster care when he was seven, and he'd mostly raised himself from that point on. He'd told her stories about the people he'd lived with, the trouble he'd gotten into, the dreams he'd had of finally finding a family that would be a *real* family to him.

She hoped that he'd found that with his wife.

"Do you have children, Logan?" she asked.

"Amanda and I planned to, but it didn't happen."

"So, you're alone?"

"I have friends and community. That's my family."

"Oh." She didn't know why hearing him say that made her throat clog and her eyes sting.

Maybe because when she'd allowed herself to think about Logan, she'd always imagined him with the big family that he'd once told her he wanted.

"Is there anyone you want me to contact for you? A girl-friend or—"

"I don't want you to tell anyone you saw me. Not your best

friend. Not a boyfriend. Not the police." He pulled into the parking lot of a well-lit hotel and parked in a shadowy corner. "You'd better get in there. The sooner you check in, the sooner you can start making the story that you told into the truth."

"Okay." But she didn't want to leave him running through the dark town, trying to find a safe place to hide. She dug through her purse, took some money from her wallet and pressed it into his hand. "Take this. You can use it to get a room somewhere else."

"I can't take your money." He shoved it back at her.

"I took your money thirteen years ago. Two thousand dollars, Logan. Remember? Consider this a partial repayment of the debt." She tucked the bills into the pocket of her husband's flannel shirt.

"There was no debt. It was a gift." He trapped her hand, his palm pressing hers against worn flannel. She felt his heart beating beneath the fabric, his warmth seeping into her palm.

"This is a gift, too, then. Take it, okay? Because I can't stand thinking about you wandering around in this storm." Her voice broke, and she looked away.

"Don't cry." He cupped her cheek so gently that she thought she might just do what he'd told her not to.

"I'm not."

"Good." He smiled and leaned across her to open the door. "Better go. The longer you sit here, the weaker your alibi gets."

Alibi?

Was she really going to need one?

She hoped not.

Prayed not.

She'd spent so much of her life in trouble, dug in so deep that she couldn't ever get out of it. Once she'd escaped, she'd promised herself that she'd never return. She'd been an upright citizen, an excellent college student. She filed her taxes on time, had never been pulled over for speeding.

Up until the past few hours, she'd never worried about seeing a police cruiser or an officer of the law. She'd always assumed that they were on the same side.

Not anymore.

She'd crossed a line, committed a felony. Probably more than one. If the police found out, she was in big trouble. It should matter a lot, but at that moment, all she cared about was making sure that Logan would be okay.

"Why don't you take my car? You can drive—"

"How will you get home?"

"I'll call a taxi."

"And if I get caught with your Jeep?"

"You won't."

"There's no guarantee of that, Laney. Just like there's no guarantee that a police officer won't pull into this parking lot and see us sitting here together. Go check into the hotel. Get a good night's sleep. When you wake up, tell yourself this was all a dream." He smiled and brushed a strand of hair behind her ear, his fingers calloused and hard.

She swallowed down further protest and climbed out of the Jeep. He was right. The best thing for both of them was to go it alone. With her cabin burning to the ground, the police would eventually track her down. If Logan were with her, they'd find him, too.

"Be careful," she threw out before she closed the door.

He nodded, his eyes dark in the dim interior, his jaw shadowed with the beginning of a beard. So different than the teenager that he'd been, but somehow just the same, too.

She hurried across the parking lot, nearly running on the snow-slick pavement.

A car door closed behind her, the soft snap echoing through her head as she entered the hotel.

Logan heading out into the storm again.

If she thought about it too long, she might turn around and go with him, so she didn't think. She just smiled at the night clerk and did her best to forget that she'd just left her best childhood friend to face his troubles alone.

FIVE

Laney's cell phone rang as she dragged her suitcase into her room. She answered quickly, her heart stuttering as an officer introduced himself, explained that her husband's cabin had burned down and asked if he could ask her a few questions.

"Sure," she said, settling onto the bed, her heart pounding so frantically she thought that she might pass out.

"Your neighbor said that you were on vacation?"

"That's right."

"And that you're staying in a hotel close to the pass?"

"About fifteen miles from it."

"Mind if I stop by? It'll be easier to conduct the interview face-to-face."

She did mind.

A lot.

"That's fine. Or I could stop by the station on my way home in the morning." She hoped she didn't sound desperate for him to take her up on the offer.

"It's better if we speak tonight. Just give me the name of the hotel and the exit number."

She had no choice, so she rattled off the name of the hotel, the exit number and her room number. She wanted to keep talking and give him information that he hadn't asked for just to try to prove that she was innocent of any wrongdoing.

Only she wasn't innocent, and he hadn't accused her of anything.

Yet.

She bit her lip, said goodbye after the officer did and disconnected. Then she sat on the bed staring at her shoes and wondering how she'd gotten into such a mess. Snow melted from her boots and seeped into the carpet, the track of slushy prints that led from the door to the bed making her pulse jump again.

Footprints.

Were Logan's near her car?

Would the officer be looking for them, trying to see if she'd arrived at the hotel alone?

She pulled open the curtain, peering out into the parking lot. Snow fell heavily, quickly filling in the tracks that she'd left. Hopefully it would fall fast enough to completely cover Logan's tracks.

Please, God, let the snow keep falling.

She rubbed the back of her neck. The officer hadn't said a word about Logan, and Laney had no reason to believe that he'd connected any dots.

She had a bad feeling, though, that he had.

Two hours and forty-five excruciating minutes later, a police cruiser pulled into the parking lot. Laney watched through the window as two officers got out. She stepped back, her mouth dry and her heart thumping.

Seconds later, someone knocked on the door.

She opened it and looked into onyx-black eyes.

"Mrs. Jefferson?"

"Yes." She glanced beyond him and saw the other officer moving toward her Jeep. Obviously, they'd run her license plate number and had been looking for her vehicle. Were Logan's tracks covered?

Please, God. Please.

"I'm Officer Daniel Kane. Washington State Police. Mind if I come in?"

"Sure. No problem." She stepped back to let him pass.

"Sorry to have to come with such bad news." He settled onto a chair, smiled easily. Disarming. Charming. Holding her attention while his partner checked her car.

"You said my husband's cabin burned. Were they able to save anything?"

"I'm afraid not."

"How about the shop?"

"The fire crew was able to keep the fire contained to the cabin."

"I'm so glad. My husband loved that shop." She tried to smile and hoped that he saw her failure as grief rather than guilt.

"He passed away a couple of years ago?"

"That's right." Obviously, Officer Kane had done his research.

"How many times have you visited the cabin since his death?" His eyes were so black she couldn't see the pupils for the iris, his face slender and a little too pretty to be handsome.

"I…" She almost slipped up. She almost told him that she'd been back for the first time that night but caught herself just before the words came out. "H…haven't."

"You were heading there tonight?"

"I planned to visit on the way to my parents' house in Green Bluff." She explained as briefly as she could. Her father's death, her inheritance, the need to move on with her life.

Officer Kane took notes as she talked, looking up every few minutes and nodding encouragingly.

When she finished, he tapped his pen against his thigh and looked her right in the eye. "Do you have insurance on the cabin, ma'am?"

"Of course." She left it at that. She might be guilty of several crimes, but she hadn't burned down William's cabin.

"What time did you leave your house?"

"I had a dinner meeting with a client at six. I stopped home to grab my suitcase and took off after that."

"So…maybe seven?"

"I'm not sure. I wasn't on any time schedule. I took two weeks off work to take care of my parents' estate and William's cabin. I'm thinking of putting my house in Seattle on the market, too. I'm just kind of playing things by ear." She was talking too much, and she needed to stop before she gave something away that she shouldn't.

"You're putting your house on the market because of financial difficulties." It wasn't a question, and Laney stiffened.

"I'm thinking of putting my house on the market because my husband and I planned to fill it with children. Unfortunately, he died before that could happen. My finances, if you really need to know, are just fine."

"Sorry." He didn't look sorry. He looked…predatory. "What time did you check in here?"

"Right before you called."

She stuck to the truth, knowing that he could easily check the facts.

"It's a two-hour drive from here to Seattle."

"It's been snowing buckets for a few hours. I stopped at a rest stop for a while hoping that the weather would clear. When it didn't, I found a hotel. I'm heading back home tomorrow."

She *had* stopped on the way to the cabin, grabbed a soda and a hot dog and stared at them while she wondered if she were doing the right thing.

"What rest stop?"

She gave him the exit number and the name of the shop

and prayed that there weren't security cameras outside the little store that she'd visited.

"All right. I think that's it." Officer Kane closed his notebook, and she thought—hoped—he might be leaving. He glanced around the room. "Mind if I use the restroom?"

"Go ahead." He wouldn't find any sign of Logan because Logan hadn't been anywhere near the room.

Logan…

She paced to the window and pulled back the curtains. The second officer was gone, probably in the lobby interviewing the night clerk. Good thing she'd told the truth about the time she'd arrived.

"I'm done here, but I'd like to take a look in your Jeep if you don't mind." Officer Kane stepped out of the bathroom.

"Why?" It was all she could think to say.

"You didn't ask how the fire at the cabin started."

She hadn't, and she probably should have.

Too late now.

"I guess I'm still in a state of shock. It's been standing for the two and a half years since my husband's death, and I can't believe that it's gone."

"Right. The thing is, someone set that fire, Mrs. Jefferson. The fire marshal has already confirmed that. It seems like quite a coincidence that you just happened to be heading to the cabin on the night it suddenly went up in flames."

"I didn't set the fire, if that's what you're implying."

"Mind if I check your car anyway?"

"Not at all."

Officer Kane walked outside.

Laney grabbed her purse, threw on her coat and followed, unlocking the Jeep door and stepping back while he searched it.

It didn't take long. As always, the Jeep was neat as a pin, just the way William had liked it. The floor mat on the driver's side was wet, and the passenger's side mat dry. Logan must have dried it off before he'd left. Any mud that might have splattered from the dirt road had been cleaned off the wheels and bumpers. Logan again. He'd been thinking ahead, planning for this moment.

Thank you, God, for that.

Trunk empty. Backseat empty. No evidence that Laney had been at the cabin. No evidence of Logan's presence. Nothing, and Officer Kane didn't look happy about it.

"I guess that's it. What are your plans after the storm blows over?"

"I'm going back to Seattle."

"I'll be in touch." He handed her a business card. "Give me a call if you remember anything that might help with the case."

"Like?"

"Anything." He waved to his partner, who was picking his way across the parking lot.

"I will."

"One more thing." Kane turned his gaze back to Laney, spearing her with his deep black eyes, and she knew exactly what he was going to say. "You used to be friends with a man named Logan Randal, correct?"

"I haven't heard from him in years." At least not until a few hours ago.

"Then you probably don't know that he's an escaped felon. We have reason to believe he was somewhere in the vicinity of your husband's cabin tonight. Is there any reason why he might want to burn it down?"

"Not that I know of, but like I said, I haven't heard from him in years."

"If you do hear from him, give me a call."

"Okay."

"Keep in mind, Mrs. Jefferson, that if you don't, you'll be aiding and abetting a felon."

"I understand."

He climbed into his cruiser, and she hurried back to the room, slamming the door and not even looking out the window to watch Officer Kane and his partner drive away.

She dropped onto the bed fully clothed, nearly jumping out of her skin when the phone on the nightstand rang.

She picked it up, sure it must be a wrong number.

"Hello?"

"You okay?" It was Logan's voice, warm and smooth as melted chocolate.

"Where are you?"

"With a friend."

"Are you—"

"We've been watching the hotel, waiting for the police to show. I wanted to make sure you weren't arrested before I took off."

"The officer asked about you. I told him it had been years since I saw you."

"Thanks."

"You don't have to thank me, Logan. I—"

"Don't say you're repaying a debt and don't say you owe me. Whatever I did for you is in the past, and whatever happens to me now, I want you to stay out of it. You stick to the story you told that police officer. Go back to your life in Seattle. Pretend you never saw me."

"Just a dream?"

"Exactly. Will you be okay to get home by yourself?"

"I'll be fine."

"Good. Get some sleep." He disconnected without saying goodbye. She blinked hard, trying to hold back the tears she'd been fighting for hours.

It was one in the morning, and she was exhausted, but

sleep didn't come. She stared up at the ceiling, listening to the silence, her heart so heavy in her chest it hurt to breathe.

She'd missed Logan.

She hadn't realized that until she'd seen him again.

Now, she felt the hole his absence had left, and she wanted to tell him that. Tell him that he'd been everything to her when they were kids.

Just in case she never saw him again.

She swiped at a tear and swallowed down more.

She'd wanted to move on with her life. Maybe this was God's way of helping her do it. Closure on every front. Her parents. William. Logan. Goodbye to all that she'd been and hello to something new and wonderful.

Only she didn't think that it could happen if Logan were in jail or worse.

What if he died because she hadn't been able to help him enough?

He'd said that he was with a friend.

Hopefully that friend could take him far away from the people who were on his trail.

She closed her eyes and tried to pray but the words wouldn't come. She kept picturing Logan as he'd been thirteen years ago, standing at the train station, watching as she'd boarded. She'd been clutching a duffel in one hand and a ticket in the other, the money he'd handed her tucked in her purse, the address and phone number of her Seattle contacts in the pocket of her jeans. Logan had already called and told the pastor and his wife that Laney was on the way. They were going to meet her train, take her home.

Just in case, he'd said when he'd given her the address and phone number. *But don't worry. They were really good to me when they were in Los Angeles. I know they'll be there for you, too.*

She hadn't needed the contact information.

Logan had done everything that needed doing to get her started on a new life.

She wished that she could have done the same for him.

Her failure hurt. It really did.

She turned onto her side and stared out the window until the snow stopped falling and she tumbled into sleep.

SIX

"Did nearly freezing to death make you stupid, Randal? First the phone call and now this. I should have driven you to Seattle like I wanted to," Darius Osborne growled as he turned onto a snow-covered dirt road. A security specialist with Personal Securities Incorporated, he'd been one of Logan's closest friends since they'd worked together on a case the previous year.

"You didn't, so there must be a reason." Logan had called Darius out of desperation, knowing that he and his new wife were spending four months in Seattle while Darius worked for a high-profile politician. It had taken less than two hours for Darius to pick Logan up at a gas station across the street from Laney's hotel and an hour longer than that for them to make it to Green Bluff.

"I thought that maybe you had a point. Who's going to look for you in the town where you were arrested, right? Now, I just think you're nuts." The truck bounced over the rutted road, snow swirling in its headlights. At least they had that—the storm of the century blowing in and covering their tracks, everyone in Green Bluff tucked safely in their beds and no one around to see Darius's vintage Ford.

"What's nuts about staying in the Mackey place? It's on

a hundred acres on the outskirts of town. Not a neighbor for miles," Logan pointed out.

"The place has been abandoned for years. No electricity. Probably no water, gas, heat."

"Laney said her father's attorney was expecting her. Everything should be turned on."

"If it's not?"

"I'll be cold."

"You wouldn't be if you'd use a little common sense and stay at my place."

"And put you and Catherine at risk? I've already pulled you into this further than I should have by asking for your help."

"You would have helped either of us."

"That's not the point."

"Then what is?"

"You and Catherine deserve a little happiness. I want to make sure you get it. Let me out here. The house is only a couple of miles away, and I can walk that far."

"I don't think so."

"Catherine will kill me if you get thrown in jail for this, Osborne. Stop the truck."

"Catherine knew the risk when you called. So did I. We were willing to take it." He drove over a small rise, the truck's headlights splashing across crisp white snow. "Sure do hope this snow keeps up. If anyone sees tracks in the Mackey's driveway, they're going to be suspicious."

"Like I said, the place is in the middle of nowhere. No one will notice the tracks."

"You can't stay there forever, Logan. What's your plan?"

"Figure out who framed me and get enough evidence to prove it."

"There's been a team of people working toward that for months. What makes you think you're going to have the success that we haven't?"

"I'm the target. Our perp won't be able to rest until he gets what he's after."

"Which is?"

"Based on what happened tonight, I'd say he wants to send me to the grave as a murderer, an escaped convict and a drug runner."

"That's a lot of hate to spill out on someone."

"Exactly."

"So, we're looking for a man with a grudge?"

"*I* am. You're going back to your wife and your job in Seattle."

"My job ends Monday. I'll be back in town that evening."

"It wouldn't hurt you to stay in Seattle a little longer."

"Yeah. It would. We're friends. I'm not going to turn my back on you."

"Look, Darius—"

"You can argue as much as you want, but I'm in this, and I'm staying in it."

"Even if that means Catherine ends up in jail? She's been through that already. You can't risk her facing it again."

"You have a point."

"I usually do."

"I see that prison hasn't damaged your ego."

Logan laughed, the sound rusty and hollow. Still chilled to the bone and shivering more than he should be so many hours after his exposure to the elements, he needed to bunk down and warm up.

More than that, he needed Darius to turn around and go back to Seattle before anyone there missed him.

"The turn is just ahead. See the mailbox on the left?" He pointed to a broken mailbox barely peeking out from the snow.

"The one lying on the ground?"

"Yeah." Logan had passed the mailbox dozens of times

over the years, watching its transformation from bright white and pristine to grimy and broken. Eventually, some punk kid had taken a hammer to it, and no one in town or out of it had cared enough to fix it.

Logan hadn't cared either.

As a matter of fact, he'd taken pleasure in seeing Josiah and Mildred Mackey's place go to ruin.

He wondered if Laney would feel the same when she returned.

Laney.

She'd sounded terrified on the phone. Lonely. Even a little sad. Or maybe he'd just heard the past in her voice, the ghosts of all that they'd lived through together, seeping through her words.

The Mackey's oversize farmhouse jutted up from the middle of the snowy yard, the old pine tree that had been the perfect escape route when Logan had been young and brash enough to not care about consequences leaning close to the front facade.

Darius whistled under his breath as he parked near the porch. "This place is huge."

"Josiah Mackey's great grandfather built a fortune on coal mining. He founded the town and owned most of it." Josiah had taken pride in that and in his reputation, his appearance and his ability to pull the wool over the eyes of the community.

It had been a pleasure to take the guy down, to see him taken away in handcuffs, his once perfectly styled hair standing up in tufts around his head.

"Josiah Mackey? Never heard of the guy."

"You were a few years too late to know him."

"The way that you're talking, I'd say that I didn't miss out on much."

"You didn't miss out on anything. Josiah was Green Bluff's

golden son. On the surface, he was a philanthropist, a savvy business man and a strong Christian. He used his reputation to swindle the government and to manipulate the system. He also used it to hide at least one murder."

"Nice guy."

"Yeah. When the people of Green Bluff realized the truth, they turned their backs on him."

"Sounds like you know a lot about the guy."

"I lived with his family for five years, and I was the one who made sure that he paid for his crimes."

"You think he might be behind what's happening to you?"

"He's dead."

"What about his wife?"

Good question. Logan had always thought of Mildred as a follower, a woman who'd gone along with her husband's schemes because he'd been stronger than she was, his personality overshadowing hers. She *had* been spiteful, though. The handprints on Laney's cheeks had always been hers. The scratch marks on Laney's arms, the bruises from pinching fingers always Mildred's.

"She went to jail for a couple of years. While she was there, she divorced her husband. That's about all I know."

"Maybe it's time to learn more."

"Maybe. Thanks for the lift, Osborne. Give Catherine my best."

"I'll be back in town Monday."

"It would be better if you weren't." He got out of the truck.

"Hold on a second. Catherine packed these for you." Darius thrust two bags into Logan's hands and dropped a backpack on top of them.

"Tell her thanks." He hurried to the front door. Locked. A lifetime ago there'd been a key under the welcome mat, but the mat was gone.

"You think you can get in?" Darius called.

"I think so."

"Maybe I'd better stick around until you do."

Logan nodded, looking up at the attic window. He'd removed the lock on it himself his very first night in the house, making sure he had easy access in and out because he'd hated being locked up. He still hated it.

It took a while to make it up through the thick pine boughs, but he managed, his arms burning and his chest heaving as he opened the attic window and dropped into the room beyond. Dark and dank and cold. Just like it had been the first night he'd slept there. He wouldn't let the memories control him, though. He ran down the attic steps and through the empty house, his feet pounding on old wood, the darkness edging in, reminding him of the years he'd spent creeping around the place.

He opened the front door, cold air blowing in and chasing away the memories.

"You sure you want to stay here?" Darius thrust the bags into his hands again.

"For now."

Darius gave a curt nod and jogged back to the truck.

Logan didn't watch him drive away, didn't second-guess his decision to come back to the house that he'd once wanted to burn to the ground. He just needed a few days to think up a plan, to make a list of suspects, to try to find some order in the chaos that his life had become. The house he'd hated would provide that.

Sometimes, the worse things we've ever lived through make us the best people we could ever hope to be.

Amanda had said that after her fifth miscarriage, her face streaked with tears as she'd told Logan that she'd wanted to adopt.

He'd held her, wiped the tears from her cheeks and told

her that they could adopt a dozen children and fill their house with laughter and family.

She'd died two months later, her life slipping away as he'd tried desperately to save it. He'd failed her and himself.

He walked into the kitchen and scrounged through the drawers until he found the key ring with the spare keys. Josiah Mackey had loved cars, and he'd kept dozens of them out in the old barn. Maybe Logan could get one of them started. Having transportation would offer options, giving him a way to run if he needed to.

For now, all he wanted to do was curl up under a blanket and sleep. He carried the bags and backpack up to the attic and lay down on the old cot that he'd spent five years sleeping on. He could have used one of the guest bedrooms or even the Mackeys' or Laney's, but he'd have a better chance of escaping from the attic if someone entered the house looking for him.

Hopefully, he wouldn't need to.

Not for a while, anyway, because right now, all he felt capable of was sleep.

The farmhouse looked the way Laney remembered it.

White clapboard siding. Black shutters. Doublewide stairs leading to a wraparound porch. Everything just a little older than when she'd lived there. A little dingier. Time hadn't spared the old Mackey place, and she was glad. The place had no magical powers. It was just a house that should have been a happy placc to grow up.

She stood in the snow-covered yard, calf deep in fresh powder. Three days of pacing her Seattle brownstone, and she'd finally decided to go with her original plan. She'd flown from Seattle to Spokane International Airport, rented a car and driven toward her old home, the key that her father's attorney had sent her a month ago heavy in the pocket of her jeans. Hopefully, Christopher Banks had also had the electricity turned on. She didn't want to spend the night in a dark, cold house.

She dragged her suitcase from the back of the rental car and made her way up the porch stairs. Her hand shook as she pulled the key from her pocket.

So many years, and she'd never had any desire to return. Even now she wanted to be somewhere else. Anywhere else.

She unlocked the door and stepped into the oversize foyer. Her great-great grandfather had built the house from the fortune he'd made. He'd chosen prime land on the Spokane River, had planted extensive orchards and made another fortune shipping apples all over the country.

Laney had heard the story a thousand times, and she'd always hated it because it had tied her family to property at the edge of a town that thought the sun rose and set on the Mackeys. More than a hundred years of charitable contributions, a church paid for and built, a youth center founded in the 1970s—all because of Laney's family. Anyone watching from the outside believed that charity and love were part of the Mackeys' genetic makeup. That faith had built a family so vital and strong that its power spilled into the community and the people who lived there.

Smoke and mirrors.

Laney knew every trick.

She shuddered, leaving her suitcase in the dust-coated foyer and walking into the living room. She flicked on the light, relieved to see that Christopher *had* done as he'd promised and had the electricity turned on.

Someone had covered her mother's prized white couch and love seat in plastic. Still not a mark on the fabric. The antique tables and lamps were coated with dust, but the place hadn't been vandalized or looted. Laney wasn't sure if she was relieved or disappointed about that.

She ran a finger over the fireplace mantel. From the time she'd been old enough to stand on a chair, she'd been responsible for dusting the wood and wiping down the Victorian tiles. She'd never minded the job. Loving the old house had been bred into her. What she'd hated was what came after. No completed job was ever good enough. No chore ever ended without harsh words or harsher punishment. Whatever her great-great grandfather's legacy of faith and giving, it had been lost in translation over the decades. Now there was nothing left of it.

Her throat tightened on the thought, her heart beating a hard, rough rhythm. If things had been different, she'd have stayed in Green Bluff, married there and raised her children in the family home.

Instead, she'd sell everything that the Mackeys had stood for. The house, the land, the history behind it all. She'd go back to Seattle and do the same with the house that William had so lovingly restored—his legacy to the children they'd planned to have together. Now it would be someone else's legacy. She'd already made up her mind about it. She had known when she'd left the hotel and driven west that she'd call the Realtor and sign the papers to list the brownstone. As much as she loved the place, it wasn't the same without William in it.

The wood creaked as she walked up the curved staircase, another hint at time passing without any attention or care being given to the old place. Her mother had hated creaky floors and musty smells. She'd seen none of the beauty and craftsmanship of the old house. She'd wanted new and modern. Only the thought of the community's reaction if the Mackey house were razed to the ground had kept Mildred from insisting that the place be torn down and built again.

Laney ran her palm along the wooden handrail that had

been carved by local artisans long before her parents had been born.

Christopher had been right. Tearing the place down because of the things that had happened in it made no sense. Someone would love the place into happiness and, maybe eventually, the place would be what it had been in her great-great grandfather's time.

A soft thump sounded from somewhere above, and she froze, her foot on the landing, her heart pounding wildly. There was nothing up there but the attic and the little room where foster kids had always stayed. One window, a rollaway cot, a closet without a door. Frigid in the winter and scorching in the summer. Dark in the deepest part of the night.

Laney had spent time in the attic.

Too much time in the overcrowded storage room, sitting in the antique tall-backed chair.

You move a muscle and I'll make you pay. You hear me?

Her mother's voice, and Laney still heard it.

She swallowed bile.

Nothing there now. Just the house settling the way old houses did.

Another thump and the hair on the back of her neck stood on end. She didn't believe in ghosts, but she felt the past pressing in. Nothing good had happened in that house. Not in Laney's lifetime.

Except for Logan.

There'd been no report on his recapture, and Officer Kane hadn't mentioned him again. Was he okay? Had his friend brought him to safety?

She wanted—needed—to know.

Thump.

Her heart skipped a beat, her blood cold with dread.

Creak.

The attic stairs. She knew the sound, having heard it thousands of times. After Logan had moved in, she'd listened for it, knowing that he was sneaking out of his room and coming to check on her.

Are you okay? He'd whispered under the locked door, and she'd felt better just knowing he was there.

She crept across the landing and stood at the attic door. Beyond it narrow stairs led up into the room that had once been maid quarters. Laney had only ever known it to be a place where kids disappeared. Troubled kids. Kids who had no one and nothing and who came to the Mackeys' place to be loved and rehabilitated.

Only there was no love in the house.

She grabbed the old-fashioned glass doorknob, her palm slick with sweat despite the cold air that seeped under the door.

Just open it, Laney. You'll see there's nothing but memories there.

She yanked the door open, a scream wrenching from her throat as a dark shadow lunged out.

SEVEN

She slammed into the wall. No breath to scream again. Clawing at the black thing that pressed in, grabbed her arm and twisted it high against her back. Just a little tighter and it would snap.

She stilled, cold with fear.

Please, God. Please!

She butted her head into a hard chin.

No spirit or demon swooping in from the past. Some*one*.

"Laney! Stop!" The growl vibrated against her ear and ruffled her hair.

She stilled, her body responding even as her mind struggled to make sense of her name and the sudden gentleness of the hand smoothing down her arm, massaging away the pain.

She felt sudden warmth where there'd been ice, and she jerked away and looked into Logan's pale face and dark blue eyes. Her legs wobbled, her body weak with relief. "What are you doing here?"

"I could ask you the same."

"It's my house. I told you I had to clean it out and put it on the market." She wanted to throw her arms around him, and that annoyed her. She'd spent years learning to be strong and independent. Even with William, she'd never allowed herself to completely rely on him. She'd maintained her career and made her own decisions about her life and how she wanted to live it. She'd loved him and all the dreams he'd represented, but she'd never allowed him to be her everything.

"I thought we agreed that you'd stay in Seattle."

"We didn't agree on anything."

"This isn't good, Laney." He ran a hand over his hair, the dark circles under his eyes speaking of sleepless nights, the pale cast to his skin alarming.

"Are you sick?" She ignored his comment, reaching out to touch his forehead and his cheek.

Logan grabbed Laney's hand and pulled it away from his cheek. She shouldn't be there. He still couldn't wrap his mind around the fact that she was.

"I was sick. I'm better now," he told her, his throat still raw from whatever bug had attacked him. He did feel better, though. About a million times better.

"You don't look better," Laney responded, her eyes shadowed, her face a shade too pale.

"You didn't see me two days ago or you wouldn't be saying that."

"Why don't you lie down in one of the guest rooms? I'll make you some tea. Have you eaten recently?"

The words poured out of Laney, and Logan wanted to press a finger to her lips and seal them in. His head throbbed, his body weak from a fever that had finally broken that morning. "Ignoring what I said won't change the truth of it."

"What?" She paused with her hand on the railing, her green eyes misty and wide, her hair a wild mass of curls around her face.

"It's not good that you're here."

"This is where *I'm* supposed to be." She hadn't said that he was the one who didn't belong, but he was pretty sure she meant it.

"Okay, then. *I'll* leave."

"Wait." She grabbed his arm, her fingers curved around his biceps, her fingers warm against his skin. Heat speared through him, so sudden and unexpected that he took a step toward her.

Her eyes widened, and she dropped his arm, obviously as surprised as Logan.

"There's no sense in you leaving now. No one knows you're here."

"People know that *you're* here, though."

"One thing has nothing to do with the other."

"You'll have visitors. That's the way this town is."

"And you'll stay hidden in the attic or in one of the bedrooms until the visitor is gone."

"I think—"

"How about we discuss it over some tea? I could really use a cup." She jogged down the steps, and he let her go. If she wanted to make tea, fine, but she wasn't going to convince him to stay.

There were seven bedrooms in the house. He knew each one. Mildred and Josiah's. Laney's. The nursery converted into an office. The four guest rooms all decorated the same. Antique bed frames, oversize armoires. Everything coated in dust and grime.

He walked into one of the rooms and sat on the bed, the history of the house alive around him. He'd spent the past three days steeped in memories of his childhood, of his time with the Mackey family, a raging fever bringing him to the edge of hallucinations. With it gone, he'd planned to tackle Josiah's cars and see if he could get one of them started so that he could get out of town.

He had a woman to find.

One he hadn't seen in thirteen years.

One who might very well be holding a grudge against him. Mildred Mackay.

The name had been rolling around in his head since Darius had asked about Josiah's wife.

"Here you are." Laney walked into the room carrying a big silver tray. A silver teapot sat in the center of it, two white porcelain mugs to either side. She set it down on the bed and handed Logan one of the cups.

"I'm not much of a tea drinker."

"I put plenty of sugar in it. Of course, maybe you've outgrown your sweet tooth."

"Not even close." He sipped the hot, sweet brew, letting it slide down his throat and warm his stomach.

"Me neither." She eyed him over the rim of her mug. "I guess I should ask you why you're here. Of all the places in the country your friend could have brought you, this seems like the worst."

"I figured the best place to hide was right under the noses of the people who are looking for me."

"You are taking a big chance. If one person had noticed that someone was here, you'd already be back in jail."

"I haven't even looked out a window. Besides, you know how lonely and isolated the farm is."

"I always thought it felt that way because of the things that happened in it. All the secrets that were forced on us. But I guess it is pretty far from everything." She smiled, her full lips trembling. "Does it seem strange to you, being back here after so many years?"

"A little. Maybe not as strange as it seems to you. I've seen the place a lot over the past decade. You haven't."

"True. It's in pretty good shape, all things considered." She wiped dust from the elaborate headboard, her palm caressing satiny wood.

"You should be able to get a good price for it."

She nodded and swallowed another sip of tea.

"That's not what you want?"

"I think it is, but this is my legacy. My family has been steward of it for over a century. It's a little harder than I thought it would be to think about ending that."

"Then keep the place."

"That's not such an easy thing to do either." She walked across the room, pulled back the curtain and let sunlight stream in.

"It's as easy as you want it to be, Laney." He stood behind her, looking out over the pastures and orchards that made up the farm. All of it was overgrown and snow covered now, but he remembered the years that he and Laney had worked the fields together, given tours of the orchards and pretended that the beauty on the outside of the house matched what was inside.

He'd done it for her.

He'd thought about running so many times, but he'd stuck it out because he couldn't imagine leaving Laney.

Now leaving her was all he could think about.

"I'd like to borrow one of your dad's old cars. Is that okay with you?"

"Do you think any of them will be working after all this time?" She turned, her body brushing his, quicksilver heat racing through him.

He stepped away, his body humming and his pulse racing.

No way would he let himself think about what that meant.

Not when there was so much riding on his ability to walk away. "It's worth a try."

"That's fine, but you'd better wait until the sun goes down. I'm pretty sure the police have been watching me these past few days, and it would surprise me if they stopped now that I'm in Green Bluff."

"Have you had trouble with them?"

"Not really. There wasn't any evidence in my Jeep, and I don't have anything at my place in Seattle that matched what was used to start the fire at the cabin. I think they suspect that I was there, but they can't prove it."

"But you think you're being watched?"

"There've been cars parked on the street outside my house in Seattle every night."

Surveillance for sure, and they'd wanted her to know it. Intimidation tactics?

"I'll wait. If I can get a car started, I may need to siphon some gas for my ride out of town."

"Whatever you need, Logan. You know that."

"We're not back to you owing me, are we?" He tucked a long strand of hair behind her ears, and his fingers lingered, brushing velvety skin, sliding through silken curls.

Big mistake.

Longing speared through him, and he knew Laney felt it. Her cheeks went pink, and she stepped back.

"I'm going to get the rest of my things out of the car. If the police *are* watching, it's best if I do what I normally would, right?" She nearly ran from the room, her feet tapping on the wooden stairs.

He followed more slowly, as anxious for some space as Laney seemed to be.

She'd left the front door open, the bitter wind blowing powdery snow from the porch into the foyer. Mildred would have hated that. The thought amused him more than it probably should have. He wouldn't find thoughts of the overly anxious and spiteful woman nearly as amusing if he found out that she was the one responsible for ruining his life.

Tit for tat?

That had seemed to be Mildred's philosophy of life.

She'd been charismatic and charming when she'd wanted to be. Her posse of friends was loyal and tight, but Mildred had also had a way of blackballing any one of those friends who'd crossed her.

Logan had crossed her big-time.

And he'd never been her friend.

As a matter of fact, he'd have been a lot happier if he could have found evidence to connect her to the death of the teenager who'd frozen out in the Mackeys' barn during a raging winter storm. Logan's interview with another foster kid who'd been there at the same time had proved Josiah's cruel abuse but hadn't implicated Mildred. She'd served less than four years in a local women's prison and had been released on good behavior after that.

He'd wanted her to spend a lifetime locked up for what she'd done to Laney, but he hadn't wanted to drag Laney into the mess, hadn't wanted her to testify against her parents or be thrown into the foster system. When she'd disappeared, her parents had done exactly what Logan had known they would—told everyone in town that they'd sent her to live with a relative because she'd been making bad choices and they were afraid for her.

By the time Logan had the evidence he needed to bring them down, Laney was eighteen. Free and clear to live her life any way she'd wanted to.

It had all been part of the plan, and it had gone off without a hitch.

Until now.

It seemed almost inconceivable that Mildred would be seeking revenge so late in the game.

He slipped into the kitchen and splashed his face with cold water, feeling better than he had in days. A little food, and he'd be ready to head out. The sooner he could do that, the better. Laney's return to Green Bluff was probably the biggest news in town since Logan's arrest and conviction. As much as he loved his adopted hometown, he knew its weaknesses. Gossip was one of them, and there was no doubt that every man, woman and child was plotting a way to be the first to welcome Laney home.

"Want something to eat?" Laney walked into the kitchen, a duffel in one hand and a paper bag in the other. Faded jeans hugged her slender hips, and a soft blue sweater peeked out from under her black parka. No makeup, but she had a hint of pink in her cheeks from the cold.

Breathtaking, and he'd never even noticed when they were kids.

"Sure. What do you have?"

"Soup and crackers. I'd offer more, but I didn't want to spend much time at the store. I was afraid people might recognize me, and I didn't feel like talking." She lifted the thick fall of hair from her neck, tying it back into a ponytail and revealing the ragged edges of a silvery scar that ran from behind her ear to her jaw. He remembered the day she'd gotten it, the pool of blood under her head. The way his stomach had churned with impotent rage as the ambulance crew lifted her to a gurney and took her away. Mildred had simpered and moaned and cried as if she'd really cared that her daughter was unconscious and hurt, but all the acting skills in the world hadn't convinced Logan. If he'd witnessed whatever had happened, Mildred would have been in jail that day, but he hadn't, and Laney had been too steeped in the abuse that she'd lived with her entire life to tell the truth.

"Soup and crackers are fine."

"I have soda, too. Root beer. You still like that?" She pulled a bottle out of the bag, and he took it from her hands. Funny how it seemed like they'd never been apart, their movements in sync as she pulled out a pot and started the soup and he grabbed glasses and filled them.

"Yeah." His voice sounded thick and rougher than he'd intended.

"The soup shouldn't take long. If you want to grab some spoons from the drawer—"

"Did you hear that?" Logan cut her off.

"What?"

"An engine."

"I didn't hear anything. Maybe it was—"

"Shh!" Logan pressed a finger to Laney's lips, and her pulse jumped, her thoughts flying away as she looked into his eyes and felt something deep in her heart open up, begging to allow him in.

It was that hole that he'd left, waiting to be filled again, but she couldn't allow it.

The rumble of a car engine, faint but growing louder, filled the silence.

"Someone's coming," she whispered.

"Go see who it is. I'll wait in the attic."

"What if—"

"No one knows I'm here. Whoever it is is coming for you. Just keep cool, and everything will be all right." Logan smiled reassuringly, grabbed his glass and jogged up the stairs.

The doorbell rang, and she jumped, dashing for the door but slowing as she neared it.

Walk, Laney. Ladies always walk.

Mildred's voice seemed to echo from the bowels of the house. So many memories, so many reasons why she shouldn't have come and why she shouldn't even consider keeping the property.

But the wood gleamed beneath layers of dust, the house echoing with more than just memories that her parents had made. Other Mackeys had lived here, loved here, filled the huge house with love and laughter.

The doorbell rang again. She peeked out the peephole and saw a uniformed officer standing on the porch. Every thought of what she could do, should do, would do, fled, her mind focused on the silence of the house, the empty feeling of it.

Had Logan made it to the attic?

Had he hidden himself away there?

The officer rapped on the wood, and she couldn't put it off any longer.

She unlocked the door and prayed that she wouldn't look nearly as nervous as she felt.

EIGHT

Cold air blew in and swept more snow across the hardwood floor. If her mother were around, she'd be in a screaming frenzy by now, the wet splotches on the dust-coated wood driving her to the brink of madness.

It was so much easier to think about that than to look into the eyes of the man who stood on the porch.

She had no choice, though.

He had crisp auburn hair cut short and blazing blue eyes, with fine lines radiating out from them.

It was not someone she knew, but his uniform—dark blue with a police badge pinned to the chest—made her stomach twist.

Great.

"Can I help you?" she asked and was happy with the steadiness of her voice and the smile she offered.

"I'm Officer Tanner Parsons with the Green Bluff Police Department. I'm here to see Laney Jefferson."

"That's me, but I just got in, and I'm in the middle of unpacking. Maybe you could come back tomorrow?"

"I'd rather speak to you today." He put his hand on the door. His stance was not aggressive, but Laney was pretty certain that he didn't plan on leaving until she let him inside and answered whatever questions he had for her.

"That's fine, then. Come on in." She led him into the parlor, wishing she'd had time to pull the plastic off the furniture. It crackled as they sat and crackled again as she shifted uncomfortably.

"I'm assuming you know why I'm here." Officer Parsons took out a notepad and pen and settled in for what Laney hoped would not be a long visit.

"You want to question me about my husband's cabin?" She knew that was not the reason, but she'd let him believe that she thought it was.

"Actually, there's something else that I'd like to discuss with you."

"What's that?"

"People around here say that you were good friends with Logan Randal when you were a kid."

"That's right."

"I guess you've heard that he escaped from a police escort that was bringing him to the state prison. An SUV ran the cruiser off the road and a gunman opened fire."

"I heard." She kept her answer pithy, afraid that if she said too much, he'd hear the truth in her tone.

"You haven't had any contact with him recently?"

"No."

He stared at her, his aqua-blue eyes seeming to see right into her soul.

Please, God, don't let him see the truth. Don't let him hear Logan.

If he did, they'd both be in jail by sundown.

"We have reason to believe that Logan was injured during his escape."

"Really?" Her voice was an octave too high, and he raised an eyebrow.

"Are you okay?"

"Yes, I just… Logan helped me when no one else would.

I hate to think of him injured and alone." True, every word, and she relaxed a little, leaning back against the sticky plastic cover.

"I'm not happy about the idea either. Here's the deal, and I'm going to give it to you straight. One of the officers who was escorting Logan to prison died. The other is clinging to life. We have him under twenty-four-hour guard, and he's been able to say a few things that lead us to believe that Logan was the target of the attack. That it wasn't an escape attempt, but rather an attempted murder."

"I—"

"We're investigating, and as the officer recovers, we're hoping his testimony will be enough to reopen the case against Logan. If you happen to see him or hear from him, give him that message, will you?"

He closed his notebook and stood.

"That's it?"

"Unless you have something that you want to share with me."

She was almost tempted to confess everything, but maybe that was the plan—make her think that he was on Logan's side, then take them both down.

"I don't."

"Give me a call if that changes." He handed her a business card and stood, looking around the once-opulent parlor. "You've got quite a place here, Mrs. Jefferson."

"It's the family estate. My father left it to me."

"I heard you're selling."

"I… That's the plan."

"You'll probably get a pretty penny for it, but if it were me, I'd hold on to the place. It's not often that a family can boast something like this." He glanced around the dusty room, and she had to bite her tongue to keep from telling him just how little her family had to boast about.

He probably already knew.

He'd known about her relationship with Logan, after all.

"It is a nice place, and I've got to get to work cleaning it out. So, unless there's something else…"

"No." But, he cocked his head to the side, seemingly listening to the house.

Don't move, Logan, and whatever you do, don't walk up or down those attic steps.

If only she could send the mental message to Logan.

"Logan was responsible for getting your father thrown in jail, wasn't he?" For someone who'd said he had nothing else to discuss, the officer sure seemed to have plenty of questions.

"That's right."

"What was your dad convicted of?"

"Fraud. Negligent homicide. Reckless endangerment. Abuse. Neglect."

"He passed away a few months ago?"

"Yes."

"And your mother?"

"I don't know." She didn't care either. A couple of years ago, Mildred had tried to make contact, but Laney had refused the overtures, turning away the private investigator who'd tracked her down.

"Interesting."

"What?" She thought she heard something move upstairs, but if the sheriff noticed, he didn't give any sign of it.

"Your story."

"You wouldn't be saying that if you were the one who'd lived it."

"You're probably right. I'd better head out. You remember what I said, okay?"

"I will."

"And, if Logan happens to show up here, keep in mind that you're harboring an escaped felon if you allow him to stay."

He walked to the front door, taking his time doing it.

She wanted to show him out but just opened the door and smiled. "Thanks for stopping by."

"Call if you need anything, and be careful. You're a long way from anyone."

His warning hung in the air as he walked down the porch stairs and got into his cruiser. Laney could hear it long after he disappeared around a curve in the road. She closed the door, locked it and slid the bolt home.

"Good job, Laney," Logan said as he walked downstairs.

"You should have waited in the attic until you knew he was gone."

"I was never in the attic. I was in the office."

"Are you nuts? What if he'd asked to search the house?"

"He didn't."

"It was an officer of the law, Logan. He could have had a search warrant. He might have—"

"*Now* you're going to lose your cool?" He pulled her into his arms, his hands sliding under her coat, their warmth seeping through her sweater.

She wanted to stay there, let her head rest on his chest and her arms wrap around his waist. She wanted it so badly that she pulled away and ran a shaky hand over her hair. "I'm not losing my cool. I'm just pointing out the obvious."

"I know Tanner. He'd have come with more than one officer if he planned to search the place."

"You know him?"

"I told you, Laney, I was deputy sheriff of the town for five years. Tanner joined the force three years ago. We've been friends since."

It made sense, and if she'd been thinking more clearly, she wouldn't have needed the explanation.

Unfortunately, thinking clearly seemed to be a problem when Logan was around. "If you were friends, how did you end up being accused and convicted of a crime you didn't commit?"

"Evidence. That's what law enforcement is all about. Gather enough of it, and you can prove someone's guilt. Even if he's innocent. There was plenty of it stacked against me. That had nothing to do with Tanner."

"He knows you were injured. He says that one of the officers who was shot is still alive."

"I'm glad. Camden Walker is a good man and a good officer."

"The sheriff also said that the officer's testimony might be enough to make them reopen your case. They believe you were the target of the attack and that someone was trying to kill you rather than free you."

"That's good news."

"My mother came up."

"I've been thinking about her, too."

She didn't ask why.

She didn't want to know.

But she *did* know, of course.

She knew exactly what Logan was thinking and what the sheriff was probably thinking.

"She tried to contact me a couple of years ago. She sent a letter with a private investigator she'd hired to find me."

"Let me guess." Logan walked into the parlor and dropped onto the sofa. "She apologized. Told you that you didn't know the entire story. That she'd been made to look like something she wasn't."

"Yes."

"That's what she said on the stand when she went to trial. She insisted that your father and I had set her up and that I'd then betrayed Josiah."

"For what reason?" Laney would have laughed if the whole thing weren't so deadly serious.

"She never said. Things were stacked against her, though. A dozen foster kids stepped forward to talk about her abusiveness. She didn't stand a chance. I just wish I could have linked her to..." He stopped.

"Nick's murder? You can say it, Logan. I read the news reports. I know what my parents did." With so many foster kids coming and going, most of them running away before they'd been in the house for a month, she hadn't thought much about Nick Lander's disappearance. He'd been just another one in the long line of troubled youth that her parents brought into their home.

She'd seen the story during the trial, though, and had looked at pictures of the field at the back edge of the property and what the cadaver dogs had discovered there. Six years after his death from hypothermia, Nick had finally been found.

"Only your father was convicted of Nick's murder. Your mother served time for neglect, but she wasn't tried for murder."

"That doesn't mean she wasn't involved. She was..." She fingered the scar on her knuckles made by an accidental slip of her mother's knife while they were working in the kitchen together.

That's what the doctors had been told.

The truth had been in Mildred's eyes, though.

It had terrified Laney. Thirteen years old. No one in the community who would believe anything but her parents' lies.

No one but Logan.

"I know what Mildred was. That's why I'm wondering where she is. What she's been up to all these years." Logan cut into her thoughts.

"I never contacted her. I didn't have any desire to reconnect."

"I wonder what her agenda was?" Logan walked to the

window and stared out into the snow-bright yard, sunlight playing in his dark hair and splashing across his face.

He'd always been handsome, but in the years they'd been apart, he'd filled out and grown up, becoming the man that she'd caught just a glimpse of the day she'd fled.

"I don't think it was anything altruistic."

"Me neither. It's curious that she waited a few years after she was released from prison to contact you, don't you think?"

"There was never any rhyme or reason with Mildred."

"When was your father diagnosed with MS?"

"I got notice about his illness a few months before Mildred's private detective showed up on my doorstep." She'd never thought about it before. Never had any reason to put the two together. Now that she had, she couldn't separate them. "You don't think that she wanted this back, do you? That maybe she knew my father was dying and thought that when he was gone, I'd let her live back here?"

"It's possible. She did love this house."

"She hated it, Logan. She thought it was old and outdated and drafty."

"She loved what it represented. Wealth. Power. Social standing." He met her eyes, and her breath caught.

She wanted to sink right into the warmth of his gaze.

She told herself not to look. Told herself that she shouldn't be noticing the way his hair curled near his collar, his broad hands, his dark blue eyes, the thick ridge of scars on his forearm.

She looked again.

It wasn't from the years she'd known him, but it wasn't fresh either.

She didn't realize she'd moved until she was beside him, her fingers running along the scars. "Did this happen in prison?"

"No. I was the first responder at a terrible car accident

a few years ago. I was trying to pull the victim out of the burning wreck." There was something he wasn't saying—she heard it in his voice and saw it in the depth of his eyes.

"Was the victim someone you knew?"

"My wife."

"Logan…" Her fingers curved around his forearm, her stomach hollow with grief. "I—"

"I've relived that day a million times, imagining a thousand different ways that I might have saved her. Every time, I see my failure. I'm not going to fail again, Laney."

"You're not—"

"I have a friend who will pick me up and drive me out of town. I'm going to call him."

"You were going to try to start one of my father's cars and leave tonight," she reminded him, ashamed that there was a part of her that wanted him to leave.

He was dangerous.

Not just the trouble that he'd brought with him.

Him. The man who thought that he'd failed his wife. Who didn't want to fail Laney. The teenager who'd grown into a man with so much integrity that he'd been convicted of a felony and still had the police department cheering for him.

"If Tanner has been here, there's a good chance the police are watching your driveway and the road that leads out of town. There's no way I'm going to be able to use one of your father's cars to get out of here."

"I could call someone. Maybe my dad's lawyer. He might be willing to help. You could hide in the backseat or trunk of his car when he leaves." It wasn't the best plan, but it might work. "Or, you could hide in the back of my rental, and I could drive you out of town."

"You don't think that driving out of town, making a quick stop and driving back will make the police suspicious?"

"We don't know that they're actually watching my house."

"They're watching." Logan rubbed the back of his neck. "There's an old gas station that backs onto your property on the went end. It closed a couple of years ago," Logan said.

"I remember it." Laney used to walk there in the summers and stand in the air-conditioned building. The owner had been an elderly man who always gave her a soda or ice cream. She'd forgotten that until now.

"I'll pack a few things and walk there."

"And do what? You said the place is closed down."

"It is, but it has four walls, and I can stay there until I come up with a better plan."

"Logan—"

The doorbell rang, and they both froze.

It rang again, and Logan stepped into the shadowy hall. "Check the peep hole."

Laney did as he commanded, looking out through the small hole, her stomach churning as she saw a stranger's face. "Who's there?" she called.

"Christopher Banks. Sorry for stopping by without calling. I'm going out of town on a business trip tonight. I just need a minute of your time before I leave."

"I—"

"This might be easier if we weren't speaking to each other through a door." Her father's lawyer sounded amused rather than annoyed, and aside from Logan's presence, Laney couldn't think of a reason to send him away. At least not one that wouldn't make him suspicious.

"I—"

Logan skirted by, his footsteps light as he jogged up the stairs.

"Just a second. These old locks can be tricky." She jiggled the knob, gave Logan a few more seconds to retreat, then unbolted the door and opened it.

NINE

Christopher Banks was tall and blond, his clothes perfectly pressed and fitted. He looked to be in his early thirties with hazel eyes and manicured hands. He also looked like an actor, handsome and fit, his smile easy and welcoming.

"Laney? It's good to finally meet you in person." He had a solid handshake.

"You, too. Come on in. The house is still a mess. I haven't had time to clean it yet." She resisted the urge to glance up at the stairs as she led him into the parlor.

"How was your flight from Seattle?" he asked as he settled onto the love seat.

"A little turbulence, but not bad. Would you like some coffee or tea? I'd be happy to make a pot." And happier to have him at the back of the house rather than at the front with Logan just above their heads.

"I'm fine." He shifted, frowning as the plastic crackled. "I should have had a cleaning crew come in before you arrived. The place could definitely use a little polish and shine." He ran his finger across the coffee table, scowling at the dust that coated it.

"There was no need. I'm happy to clean it myself before it's listed."

If she allowed it to be listed.

She couldn't believe that she was seriously considering the alternative—owning it, accepting her legacy. Maybe she could do better than her parents had in the house her great-great grandfather had built.

"If you change your mind, let me know. I·work a lot of estate cases, and I have a good crew that can be in and out in a few hours."

"I'll keep that in mind." The floor above their heads creaked, the sound so subtle Laney might not have noticed it if she hadn't known that Logan was there. Her cheeks heated, but Chris didn't seem to notice. He was busy pulling several file folders from a dark leather briefcase.

"Now, on to business. I have some news for you, and I think you're going to be happy about it. There are already five offers on this property."

"It's not even on the market."

"A few developers have been coveting this land for years. I put out the word that your Realtor would be willing to entertain offers before it was listed *if* the offers were worthwhile. These are."

"I'm not sure that I want to sell it to a developer." If she did, she knew the house would be torn down and the land would be split into small parcels and dotted with cookie-cutter homes.

The thought clogged her throat, and she swallowed hard.

"No?" Chris looked up from the folders that he was spreading out on the table.

"I was thinking that a family would be nice. Someone with children or grandchildren who could enjoy the orchards."

"That's a nice dream, Laney, but dreams usually aren't lucrative. Most families couldn't pay nearly what a developer could." He jabbed at one of the folders with a well-manicured finger. "This is probably the most interesting of the offers. The guy who made it owns a car dealership in Spokane. He's interested in buying the land and your father's car collection."

"I don't think any of those cars run."

"Larry is offering—" he lifted the folder and riffled through it "—forty-thousand dollars for the cars alone, and that's *as is*. I came out here a few days ago and took some pictures of the cars in the garage, then I had my staff do a little research. It seems to me that you could do a lot worse. Of course, the final decision is yours." He slid the folder toward her.

"I don't know." She took the folder reluctantly and glanced at the cover page. The seven-figure amount that the car dealer was offering was more than she'd expected, but she didn't feel any more excited about letting go of the family home. "I'm going to need some time to think about it."

"I'll be back tomorrow night. If you have any questions before then, my partner will be happy to answer them. He's in our Seattle office, but I faxed him a copy of all the offers earlier today."

"I appreciate it." The floor creaked again, and Chris looked up.

"We should probably have someone in to inspect the foundation before the house goes on the market. It sounds like it's doing a lot of settling, and I wouldn't want to be under contract and then find out that there's a problem."

"Good idea." She resisted the urge to laugh, hysteria bubbling up from the depth of her fear. If Chris discovered Logan, would he feel obligated to contact the police? Or would he be obligated to keep his silence, client confidentiality sealing his lips?

"I'll call your Realtor and see if she has a recommendation."

"I don't mind—"

"It's not a problem, Laney." He smiled and stood. "Now, if you don't mind, before I go, I'd like to take a few photos of the property. We had a query from a guy who lives out of state. He has a cousin in the area and heard about the sale—"

"A lot of people seem to be hearing about it."

"Like I said, I put the word out. It spread like wildfire. You know how small towns can be."

"I guess I do."

"If we play our cards right, we could be accepting a very lucrative offer by early next week." He pulled a digital camera from his pocket, and Laney's heart nearly leaped out of her chest. Was he planning to walk outside and take the photos? Inside?

Either way, she didn't like it. The sooner he left, the happier she'd be.

"I'd rather you wait until I clean things up."

"I'm sure that he's not worried about what shape the house is in. He's interested in the property itself. He has plans to build a shopping center here if he wins the bid."

A shopping center standing in the same spot where generations of her family had lived?

The rational side of Laney knew that she should rejoice in the thought, but all she could do was picture the golden fields of wheat paved with asphalt.

"I'd be happy to take the photos myself tomorrow morning. I can email them to you or to the interested party," she insisted, and Chris finally conceded.

"I guess that will have to be okay. Look over the offers. We can meet when I get back from my business trip to discuss them further. I'll bring any other offers then."

"I appreciate it."

Laney walked out of the parlor with him, something nagging at the back of her mind.

Logan's words. Officer Parson's. They had both asked about Laney's mother.

"Chris, I was wondering if my father left anything to my mother in his will?"

"Your mother? No."

"So you didn't contact her after my father's death?"

"They'd been divorced for ten years when he died, and you were listed as Josiah's next of kin."

"I know. I just...wondered."

"Would it make you feel better if he had left her something? If he'd wanted me to contact her?"

"I—"

"It can't be easy to have been raised by parents who loved each other but who couldn't make it through tough times together."

"I haven't been part of either of their lives in more than a decade. Their divorce hasn't affected me at all," she said truthfully.

"Really? Your father always spoke fondly of you. He called you a blessing from God."

"That's a shock, Chris, because the only thing he ever called me to my face was 'worthless.'" More truth, and Chris didn't seem happy about it.

"You were a child. Your perception may have been skewed."

"Do you live in Green Bluff?"

"Yes."

"But you didn't grow up here?"

"I moved here from Seattle a couple of years ago to open a new branch of my law firm."

"Then all you know about my family is what my father told you. I wouldn't take a whole lot of stock in it, considering that he spent the last ten years of his life in jail."

"You've got a point." Chris flashed his easy smile, and Laney wanted to return it. Her lips felt stiff, though, and her heart was beating oddly. Talking about her family wasn't something she liked to do, especially not with a virtual stranger.

"The reason I was asking about my mother was because I was thinking about…getting in touch with her."

"Well, I'm sure that if you want to do that, you can."

Gee. Thanks.

"If you have any information about her—"

"I don't, but I'd be happy to see what I can find out. I'm sure it won't be difficult to find her, if you really want me to."

"I do."

"No problem. I'll get started as soon as I get back."

"Thanks, Chris."

"Do read through the offers that I brought over. I'll email other offers as they come in. Send me the photos once you take them."

"I will," she said a touch too cheerfully. She didn't feel cheerful. As a matter of fact, she was feeling a little sick. The stairs creaked, and she jumped, her gaze on Christopher's back as he walked down the porch stairs.

Please, don't turn around. Don't turn around. Don't!

He turned, his eyes probing the area beyond Laney. Was Logan there?

She didn't dare look.

He smiled, waved and kept walking.

Thank you, Lord. Thank you.

She closed the door and leaned her back against it as if Chris might suddenly barge back in.

"That took a while." Logan walked down the stairs, a backpack slung over one shoulder, his long legs hidden by loose cargo pants. He'd tucked the cuffs into snow boots that looked like William's and had his left hand in the pocket of a coat that *was* William's. He filled it out more, his shoulders straining the seams.

She looked away, uncomfortable with the comparison.

"Chris had several offers on the property. He wants me to make a decision by next week."

"Make it when you're ready and don't worry about what he wants."

"I know you're right. I just…"

"Don't know if you want to sell and don't know how to tell him?"

"Don't know if I *should* tell him. The way I feel is probably just some passing phase."

"You're selling yourself short, Laney." He nudged her chin up, and her stomach flipped as she looked into his eyes. "You've never been fickle or indecisive. If you're thinking about keeping the house, there's a good reason for it."

"If there is, I can't think of one. I haven't thought about this place in years. I hated it when I was here. I've got no reason at all to keep it."

"It's a beautiful house on a stellar piece of land, and your family has lived here for generations. Isn't that enough?"

"Maybe."

"If it were me, I'd want it." He touched the handrail. "Not because of what it was when I was in it, but because of what it represents."

"That's what you said about my mother. That she might have tried to contact me because she was hoping to be part of what this house represents again."

"Yeah, but if Mildred wanted it, it would have been because she thought it meant power and prestige. I'd want it because of what it could be. A place for kids and family and friends to gather. A place full of laughter and happiness." He smiled, and her heart melted for him, every memory of every dream that he'd ever shared with her filling her heart until she thought she'd drown in it.

Her pulse pounded behind her eyes, her throat tight and

raw with a hundred things she wanted to say but couldn't. She'd wanted so much when she was kid, and Logan had wanted the same. Family and love and home. They were four years apart in age, eons apart in experience, but in that one way they had been exactly the same.

It seemed that they still were.

"Give yourself a little time to decide if the bad memories that you have are enough to chase you away from something that could be great," he continued quietly, "I'd better get out of here. The sun is already going down, and the temperature is going to drop when it does. I'll go out the back door. Lock up when I'm gone, okay?"

She followed him to the kitchen, shoving packages of crackers and cookies into his backpack. She grabbed coffee from the supplies she'd brought and shoved it in there, too.

"Do you still have the gun?" she asked as he opened the back door, the setting sun turning his dark hair chestnut.

"Yes."

"And ammunition?"

"Stop worrying, Laney. I'll be fine." He flashed his smile again, and she wanted to cry as the door closed.

She walked to the window that looked out over the backyard, watching as he made his way toward the woods that abutted her property.

Keep him safe, Lord. She prayed silently, the house settling around her, every creak and groan reminding her that she was alone.

She knew what she needed to do. Start packing things up. Whether she sold the place or not, it needed to be done. She couldn't live there surrounded by her parents' things.

She pulled her hair into a high ponytail, opened one of the cherrywood cupboards and stared at her mother's fancy white china. She'd broken one of the plates once and had been dragged screaming up to the attic and was locked in for hours. Darkness had come. Shadows had filled the storage area. She'd been maybe five or six and absolutely terrified.

She hated the memory and the china, but did she really hate the house?

Maybe not.

She glanced out the back window one last time, and then slowly tossed every bit of china into the trash.

TEN

Logan heard the engine first.

Not a car. Too rough for that.

He eased to the ground, taking cover behind a fat spruce as he scanned the area. Nothing close by. But something was coming.

Darkness shrouded the woods, casting long shadows through the trees. He waited, listening as the engine died and the forest fell silent.

He saw the light next.

He watched it bounce through the trees about a half mile from his position.

It had been years since he'd explored the Mackey property, but he tried to map it out in his head and imagine the area where the lights had appeared. A country road bisected the woods, and he thought that might be where the lights had come from. Snowmobiler, maybe?

Logan wanted to believe it.

But didn't.

He'd walked at least a mile already, and the light was between him and Laney's house.

Not good.

Logan jogged back the way he'd come, his heart thudding painfully, his mind shouting that he was failing again, that by the time he made it back to the farmhouse, the person with the light would already be there.

Laney might be dead before he reached her.

He shoved the thought away, not allowing himself to dwell on it.

He wouldn't allow himself to remember the way she'd looked when they'd been standing in the foyer, her face soft and open and filled with emotion. Their shared dreams had been in her eyes, and he'd had to leave or he might have started wondering what it would be like to work toward those dreams together instead of separately.

No more love. No more entanglements. That had been his motto since Amanda's death. He'd refused to get close enough to anyone to risk his heart, to risk another failure.

But he *was* close to Laney, their shared past serving as a foundation that seemed sturdy enough to build just about anything on.

The engine roared to life again, and Logan cocked his head to the side, listening as it faded away.

He should have been relieved, but he felt tense and anxious, his nerves alive with adrenaline. He scanned the forest again and caught sight of a single light slowly weaving through heavy pine boughs.

It was not moving toward the road, but toward Laney's house.

He wanted a cell phone, an ATV, a way to warn her or a way to beat the threat to her.

He didn't have either, so all he could do was run.

The first few months after William's death, Laney had been lonely, the empty house echoing the throbbing pulse of her grief. It hadn't taken long, though, to get used to being alone. She'd found that she enjoyed the silence, the space, the freedom from the emotional connection that marriage demanded.

She'd loved William; she really had. He'd been everything she'd ever wanted in a husband—kindhearted, even tempered, a good friend. He'd filled a void in her heart that had been empty for so many years, she'd barely realized it needed filling until she'd met him.

So what if her heart hadn't skipped a beat every time he walked into a room? They'd had mutual goals and faith and affection for one another, and it had been enough. More than enough.

After his diagnosis, he'd told her that she'd been his one true love. He'd said it again and again during the months of chemo and radiation. She hadn't known if it was true. She'd thought that maybe he'd just wanted that kind of love before he died.

She hadn't *ever* wanted it.

And she knew that she never *would* want it.

That kind of love could only lead to disappointment. True and deep and lasting.

She'd had enough of that to last a lifetime.

Somehow, though, as she sat in the silent parlor and looked through the offers Chris had left, she felt lonely. She yearned for someone to be sitting beside her, going over the information with her, listening as she listed all the reasons why she really should sell the property.

Someone?

Logan.

She could admit it to herself.

He was an old friend, part of her childhood, so it made sense that she'd want him around as she decided what to do with her inheritance.

She didn't *need* him around, though.

She refused to ever need anyone the way she'd once needed parents who loved her.

The china set that she'd thrown in the trash can was the first step to moving on from the nightmare she'd lived as a kid. She needed to take the next.

She just wasn't sure what it was supposed to be.

Or maybe she did.

The easiest thing to do, the best thing, would be to start cleaning and organizing. She could plan everything else as she went. Maybe after she'd removed the century's worth of Mackey stuff from the house, selling it wouldn't feel so much like betraying family.

Family?

Ha!

As if she'd had that.

She rubbed the bridge of her nose as the teakettle whistled. A cup of hot tea with plenty of sugar. That would cure a multitude of troubles. That's what the head waitress at the diner she'd worked at during college had said. Probably, she was right. A little warmth. A lot of sugar. That would help.

Knowing that Logan was safe. That would help, too.

She glanced at the clock as she poured hot water over a tea bag. He'd been gone a half hour. He should be close to the gas station by now.

She was tempted to get in her car and drive there just to make sure that he had made it.

As a matter of fact, she didn't see any reason why she shouldn't. There were a few things she could pick up from the store. Milk. Eggs. Chocolate. Blankets. Water. If she happened to drop a few of those things at the old gas station, who would know? She'd just have to be careful. Make sure she wasn't followed.

She grabbed her purse, flicked off the foyer light, then thought better of it and turned it back on. The last thing she wanted to do was return to a dark house. The place was too quiet as it was, the silence thick and heavy.

She opened the door and stepped out onto the porch, the floorboards sagging beneath her feet. She'd have to hire contractors to do some of the work around the house. A little upkeep, and the place would look fantastic. She could buy a rocking chair for the porch. Better yet, a hanging swing. In the spring, she'd get baskets of flowers to hang from the porch eaves.

No. She wouldn't because she *was* selling the house. Just like she'd planned from the very beginning. Sell it and use the money to buy a smaller property in Seattle. A modest 1920s Craftsman-style bungalow that she could make into her own. Maybe she'd get a dog or a couple of cats or both.

A soft sound drifted through the darkness—the crunch of snow underfoot. Not hers. She stopped, cocking her head to the side and listening.

"Hello?" she called, hoping it was Logan returning. He'd probably realized it was too cold to be walking and had turned around…

She didn't see the shadow move and didn't know it had come to life until she hit the ground, lungs wheezing with the effort to breathe, her screams nothing more than whimpers of air whispered into the coldness.

"You want to die tonight?" The question ruffled the hair near her ear, and she shook her head, unable to force words past her throat.

"Then you're going to do exactly what I say."

She nodded, breathless and numb.

Logan had warned her. He'd told her to stay in Seattle. She hadn't listened, hadn't wanted to believe that she was really in any danger. Maybe she'd dug her own grave.

"Into the house." He yanked her to her feet, his hand so tight on her wrist, she thought the bone might break.

"What do you want?"

"I ask the questions. You answer. That's the way the game is played." He shoved her, and she fell into the wall, her head slamming against old plaster, stars dancing in front of her eyes.

"What questions?" she asked, her mouth cottony with fear and her heart racing with it.

Please, Lord, help me.

"I told you! I ask the questions." He slapped her hard, the sudden sharp pain clearing her head. Ski mask. Gloved hands. Tall, hulking figure. A stranger shoving her backward into the house, and she was helpless to stop him.

Don't panic. Think!

She looked into cold black eyes and saw her own death in them, but she didn't say a word. She didn't move. Didn't barely breathe as she waited for his game to continue.

"Good girl," he crooned, the ugly cadence of his voice making her skin crawl. "Let's go where it's a little more comfortable." He shoved her again, and she nearly fell into the parlor.

She caught her balance on the wall, hating the gasping sound of her breath and the way her hands shook. She turned to face her attacker, backing away as he moved in close.

"You have a friend I need to talk to," he said, his black eyes staring into hers. If he had pupils, she couldn't see them, and that scared her almost as much as his ski mask. "Logan Randal. You know the name, right?" A gloved knuckle raked down her cheek, the cold leather chilling her.

"Yes."

"He visited you in your husband's cabin."

He knew about her, but she didn't have to admit anything. "No."

"Yes." He slapped her again, and she stumbled back and saw the gleam of the fireplace poker.

All she had to do was get to it.

She clung to the plan as she struggled to her feet. She'd been beaten before. Viciously. The bruises were always hidden by long sleeves and long pants. She knew how to take a blow, but this guy wasn't her father or her mother. He didn't have punishment on his mind. He'd kill her once he got the information he wanted, and she had no intention of letting that happen.

"He visited you in the cabin. You gave him a ride off the mountain. Where did you take him?"

"To a hotel," she said, stepping away. One step, two, three. How far before she backed into the hearth?

"Where?"

She gave the exit number, the hotel name, the truth, because Logan wasn't where she'd left him, and it wouldn't matter if her attacker went there.

"What happened to him after that?"

"I don't know."

"You're lying." Another slap. Her ears rang with it, the metallic taste of blood filling her mouth. She didn't dare touch her cheek.

"I'm not."

"Then how about we take a little drive? Go to that hotel and ask the manager when Randal checked out?" He grabbed her arm, his fingers digging into flesh, the feverish gleam in his eyes making her knees week.

She knew the look. She had seen it dozens of times before in her mother's eyes.

Malice. Sick enjoyment.

If she left the house, she'd never return. If she allowed herself to be driven away, she'd disappear. Just one more missing person.

"Move!" He yanked hard, digging his thumb into her wrist bone, grinding down until tears burned behind her eyes.

She didn't let them fall, willing herself to ignore the pain the way she had when she'd been a helpless kid trying to forget that her parents seemed to hate her.

She wasn't a kid anymore.

She wasn't helpless.

He dragged her further away from the parlor, the fireplace, the poker.

Do something!

She turned into him and dug her thumb into his pupilless eye. He swore, his grip loosening as he shoved her hand.

She yanked away and lunged for the poker, her hand closing around cool metal and her heart thundering as she swung with all her might.

ELEVEN

Distraction.

Exactly what Logan needed and exactly what Laney's wild swing of the fireplace poker offered. She put her strength in it, but her attacker yanked her arm forward, throwing her off balance and stopping the poker's momentum.

Now!

Logan dove into the room, slamming into the masked man and knocking him sideways.

Laney screamed.

"Run!" he shouted, but he didn't know if she listened because he was too busy avoiding swinging fists to notice.

He grabbed the guy's collar and twisted it until he cut off air.

"You're choking me."

"You think I care?"

"I can't breathe!" The guy gagged, but Logan just kept twisting.

Eventually, the masked man got the message.

He slumped, his arms and legs still.

"That's better." Logan rolled him onto his stomach, grabbed his arm and yanked it up hard enough to hurt but not quite hard enough to break. "Who sent you?"

"None of your business, jailbird."

"I think it is."

"And I think you're out of luck. You can't call the cops on me. You can't do much but stand here threatening to break my arm."

"I can do a lot more than that, punk." Logan pulled the gun he'd been carrying since he'd left the cabin and pressed it to the man's temple.

"Logan…" Laney's voice trembled, but he couldn't allow himself to be distracted. Not until the guy was trussed up like a turkey and helpless to fight. "Get me something to tie him up."

"Will duct tape work?" She moved closer. Bruises stained her left cheek, and Logan thought that maybe a quick jerk of her attacker's arm might teach him what it meant to be helpless and hurt. He resisted the urge. He might not be an officer of the law, but he still felt like one and still believed in the things he'd stood for when he'd been deputy sheriff.

"It should. Go on and get it, okay?" he said, his voice gentle, his tone easy. She looked terrified, and he needed her to know that things were under control. That she was safe. That he planned to keep her that way.

She nodded and ran from the room.

He pressed the gun a little tighter to her attacker's head, then felt the guy still, maybe afraid for the first time since he'd entered the house.

"I wouldn't mind blowing your brains out. You know that, right?" He kept his voice low and his grip on the guy's wrist tight.

"You're a cop."

"I was one. I'm not anymore."

"Then you're just too much of a coward to pull the trigger."

"You want to bet on it? Tell me who sent you."

"I don't know."

Logan released the safety on the gun. "You're sure?"

"My boss, okay? Luke Martin."

"Who is he?"

Silence, and Logan nudged him with the handgun.

"I asked you a question."

"Militia leader."

"What's the name of your group?"

"Cascade Mountain Men," he muttered.

"I've heard of it." But not of Martin. The group was closer to Seattle than Green Bluff, and their headquarters were about a hundred miles southwest of town. It was not a problem that Logan had ever had to deal with. "Why'd your boss send you?"

"He wanted me to get some information."

"About me? I guess you got it."

"I have the tape." Laney walked back into the room, and Logan locked the safety again, keeping the gun pressed against the masked man's temple.

"Start with his ankles."

"Me?" Her voice squeaked and her face was as pale as paper.

"He won't give you any trouble. Will you?"

No response, so Logan ratcheted up the pressure on the guy's arm, making sure he was too afraid of having it snap to move.

"Done," Laney finally said, her voice airy and weak.

Logan shoved the gun back in his pocket, then twisted her attacker's other arm back. "What's your name?"

Silence again.

Apparently the guy thought that he was safe as long as Laney was in the room.

He was safe anyway. No way would Logan have pulled the trigger. No matter how tempting it might have been.

He wrapped duct tape around the guy's wrists, then rolled him onto his back.

"Your name?"

The guy spat through the hole in the ski mask.

"Spit again and I'll knock you out," Logan muttered, tearing the mask from his face and looking at a stranger.

Blond hair. Black eyes that were both piercing and empty.

Logan patted him down, pulling a cell phone from one pocket and a wallet from another and sliding an eight-inch boning knife from a sheath on his calf. The blade gleamed, sharp enough to cut through flesh like it was butter.

Laney's eyes widened, the darkening bruises on her cheek red-purple against her pale skin. An image of Laney as she'd been a decade ago, her eyes red from tears and her legs covered with welts, flashed into his head.

He'd promised himself that he would get her out from her parents' home and away from their abuse. He'd sworn that he wouldn't let her ever be beaten again. That he'd protect her and make sure she had the kind of life she deserved.

He'd failed.

The same way he'd failed Amanda.

That's how it felt. No matter how many times he told himself that Laney was an adult, responsible for herself and capable of making her own decisions, he couldn't shake the feeling that he'd done this to her. Brought his trouble into her life and created chaos out of the normalcy that was all she'd ever wanted.

He tucked the knife into his boot and tried not to think about what would have happened if he hadn't returned to the house.

He opened the wallet and pulled out a driver's license.

Ronald Danvers from Tacoma. He dropped it onto the ground. The police could deal with Danvers. He wanted to be out of town, and he wanted it yesterday.

"Grab whatever you think you might need for the next few days, Laney. We're getting out of here."

"What—"

"You have an overnight bag?"

"Yes."

"Grab it and come right back."

She nodded and ran upstairs.

"You can't just leave me here," Danvers said, the edge to his voice almost enough to make Logan smile. Leaving was exactly what Danvers didn't want them to do. He probably had an accomplice waiting somewhere and a predetermined time to meet up again. That would explain the vehicle that had driven away—a drop off and a pick up.

Only Danvers wouldn't be there and Logan didn't want his partner showing up at the house. Not while Laney was there.

"Sure I can," he said, moving away from the prone man.

"Too chicken to stick around and ask the questions you need answers to?"

"Too smart to think you got here on your own," Logan replied.

Danvers didn't blink, his cold black eyes giving nothing away.

It didn't matter. Logan knew the truth, and he didn't plan to wait around. He dialed 911 on Laney's landline, giving his name and location, knowing that would get the police moving in fast. Let them come. He'd be long gone.

So would Laney.

He might not have wanted to involve her, but she was involved, and there was nothing he could do to change that.

"I'm ready." Laney reappeared, a duffel in her hand and her purse over her shoulder.

He let the phone drop as the 911 operator asked him to stay on the line. "Come on."

Laney wanted to do what Logan asked, but her legs felt stiff and heavy and her body numb. Probably her cheek and jaw should ache, but she felt nothing.

Her gaze dropped to the man on the floor, her mind jumping back to the moment when Logan had pulled the knife from his boot.

She could have been killed with it.

Easily.

She shuddered.

"It's okay. Everything is going to be fine." Logan tugged her coat closed and brushed hair from her cheek.

Would it?

She didn't know, but she had no choice but to follow him out of the house and to her rental car.

"Where are the keys?" Logan asked, and she dropped them into his hand, waiting while he unlocked the door and then climbing into the passenger seat. She was doing everything as if it were the most natural thing in the world. As if she hadn't just been attacked, beaten, nearly killed.

"Where are we going?"

"To find a ride out of town."

"We have a ride," she pointed out, her voice still shaky. Her entire body shaky. She'd almost been killed, and now she was on the run with a man wanted by the police.

"This is a rental, Laney. The police will spot it before we get a mile from your place."

"We're not going to steal a car, are we?" she asked, half convinced that that was exactly what Logan planned.

"No. I'm going to call a friend of mine. I hate to involve him more than he already is, but I don't have a choice." He pulled onto the old dirt road that bisected Laney's property and connected the highway and an old, seldom-used country road.

"I have my cell phone." She dug it out of her purse, but Logan shook his head.

"I don't want any connection between you and my friend. No hard evidence that he has had any contact with me. Otherwise, he might end up in jail. We'll use a pay phone. That way, the police might be able to prove that he got a call, but they won't know who it was from."

"Right." She hadn't thought about that. Apparently she hadn't thought about a lot of things.

He pulled into a convenience store parking lot, jumped out and used a payphone. She waited, the sound of sirens drifting into the car. The police would be at her house soon. How long before they started hunting for her and Logan?

Or were they already doing that?

Officer Parsons had been at the house earlier. He'd seen her rental car, and he probably had written down the license plate number.

A police car sped by, sirens blaring and lights flashing. Laney's heart skipped a beat. It skipped another one when Logan got back in the car.

"I'm going to park around back."

"Park?"

"We're changing rides, but it's going to be a couple of minutes before our transportation gets here. I don't want the car to be visible from the road." He pulled around to the back lot and parked in dark shadows at the edge of the pavement. Laney would have been happy to stay there, hidden by darkness and cocooned in the warmth of the car.

Logan had other ideas.

He got out, opened her door, grabbed her duffel and pulled her from the car.

"Wouldn't it be better—"

"Trust me, okay? I'm not going to let anything happen to you." He led her around the side of the building. Lone bulbs glowed above restroom doors. Other than that, the area was dark.

Laney shivered, sinking back into the shadows and stepping straight into Logan's arms. It was not an intentional thing, but it felt so right she almost stayed there.

"Sorry." She eased away, stopping short when his hands slid around her waist. "What—?"

"A police cruiser just drove into the lot."

"Where?" She would have turned to look, but he caught her chin and held her still.

"Don't. Every officer in town knows me. I need to make sure that he doesn't see my face." He bent his head, maneuvering so that his back was to the lot, her body hidden by his. His eyes glowed sapphire in the dim light, and her heart leaped in response.

What if he *was* seen?

What if the police officer approached and demanded that he surrender?

She tensed.

"Relax. This is just an ordinary night, and we're just an ordinary couple making a pit stop on the way to forever," Logan murmured, his hand sliding up her spine and tangling in the end of her ponytail.

"What if he comes over?" she responded, her voice shaky and a little too loud.

"He won't."

"But—"

"He's not here for us. He's probably on his way home after a long day and wants to grab a snack."

"You can't know that."

"No, but I *can* know that if you don't stop acting so terrified, he'll notice. If that happens, he'll come over. Then, we're both sunk," Logan whispered, pressing his forehead to hers, his eyes blazing.

"Are you sure he didn't already notice us?" She tried to relax, she really did, but the urge to turn and look was nearly overwhelming.

"He's heading into the convenience store. Don't give him a reason to change his mind." He cupped her face, his palms cool and rough, his fingers playing in the soft hair near her ears.

It felt good, so good, to have him there with her, and all the terror and horror of the attack seemed to want to spill out right at that moment, drip down her cheek and drop off her chin.

She didn't dare brush it away. She didn't want the officer to know she was crying. If he did, he'd probably feel obligated to make sure that she was okay.

"Are you in pain?" Logan wiped the tears away, his palm rasping against bruised flesh.

"No. Yes. I don't know."

"I wish that I'd gotten there sooner. He really did a job on you." He trailed a finger along her throbbing jaw.

"You saved my life. That's what matters."

"I still wish that I—" His gaze jumped to the right, his mouth tightening.

"What? Is he—"

She didn't have time to finish the question; Logan dragged her forward, his lips slamming over hers. There was nothing gentle about the kiss, and she stiffened. She should have moved away, but his lips were warm and seeking, his hands sliding along her arms, linking with hers, palm to palm. Every beat of her heart seemed to throb for him.

She lost herself in that, moving in closer and allowing the sweetness of his kiss to steal everything else away.

"He's gone." Logan pulled back, his voice hoarse and his hand shaking as he smoothed a lock of hair from her cheek. "Sorry about that. He was looking our way, and I thought that he planned to come over."

"It's okay." She stepped back, her heart pounding and her breath heaving and all the reasons why it *wasn't* okay filling her head.

She felt it too deeply.

She wanted it to continue too much.

She pushed the thoughts away, sealing them in where she kept her deepest secrets and longings.

This was Logan, after all. An old friend. A man who'd saved her life more than once and whose life she'd saved. That sort of thing created a bond. A deep one. There was no sense trying to deny it.

But the kiss had been nothing more than a means to escape detection. If she kept that in mind, she wouldn't lose any more of her heart than she already had.

A dark truck pulled into the parking lot, flashed its lights twice and drove back out onto the road.

"That's our ride." Logan took her hand, and it seemed like the most natural thing in the world to cling to him as they walked around the side of the building, cut through a field and stepped out onto the country road that led to her parents' place.

She could still hear sirens, the faint sound reminding her that the life she'd been living was over. She couldn't go back to Seattle. Not now. Until Logan's name was cleared and the men who were after him were captured, she was safer with him than alone.

"There he is. Come on." Logan broke into a jog, and she had to keep pace with him. She was clutching his hand, after all. Holding on as if he were her lifeline.

Stupid.

Because she'd become that to herself long ago. She'd loved William, but she'd never needed him the way some of her friends seemed to need their spouses. She'd always known that if something happened and she were on her own, she'd be fine. Life had taught her how to go it alone, and she'd learned the lesson well.

Now she was allowing herself to be dragged through the

darkness, picked up and nearly tossed into the backseat of an extended cab pickup. She had a quick impression of firm muscles and heat, and then Logan was shoving in beside her, his thigh pressed close to hers as he crowded close.

"Hey!"

"Save your protests for after we're on the road." Logan fumbled for her seat belt, and she shoved his hands away.

"I can manage." She snapped the belt into place and leaned a little away, trying to put some distance between them.

Not that distance was going to help.

She could still taste his kiss on her lips and feel the heavy thud of her heart.

She touched the bruises on her cheek and jaw, hoping it would remind her of all the reasons why she could never allow herself to completely give her heart to someone. She'd been bruised so many times as a kid, battered, cut, even burned, but the worst that she'd suffered was the emotional coldness and neglect, the complete lack of connection, affection and love.

By the time she'd left home, she'd learned to hold back pieces of herself, make sure that only she was responsible for the care and keeping of them. Even with William, she hadn't given everything. There'd always been a tiny part of her heart that she held in reserve.

"I'm assuming you're Logan Randal and Laney Jefferson. If not, I'm afraid that you jumped into the wrong vehicle," the driver said, his gravelly voice as dry and raspy as sandpaper. She couldn't make out his hair or eye color, but his face was all sharp angles and strength.

"If you're Seth Sinclair, we're in the right place," Logan responded as they turned onto a narrow dirt road.

"Guess we're all where we need to be. Darius asked me to stick around, offer a little protection once I get you to the safe house."

"Did he tell you that I'm wanted by the police?"

"He did. He also told me that you didn't commit the crime you've been accused of. Of course, every criminal says that."

"If you think I'm a criminal, why help me?"

"I trust Darius. If he says you're innocent, you are. Of course, my word and his don't mean squat. What you need is proof. You have anything to go on? Maybe something the police missed?"

"I have a driver's license that I pulled off the guy who attacked Laney. I've already given the name to Darius. He's doing some research."

"Anything else?"

"Nothing to write home about."

"Then I guess we've got our work cut out for us."

"There's no need for you to get involved. The last thing I want is to pull more people into my troubles. Once you get Laney to the safe house, I'm going to take off."

"And go where?" It was the same question Laney wanted to ask, and she watched as Logan ran a hand over his hair and rubbed the back of his neck.

He didn't know.

Stumped was not a good thing to be when people wanted you dead.

She touched his hand, her finger grazing his knuckles, her pulse jumping with the quick, sharp jolt of electricity.

It was a mistake, and she should have pulled away, but Logan turned his hand and captured hers, and no matter how much she told herself that she should, she couldn't quite bring herself to break the connection.

TWELVE

Two hours, thirty-five minutes and ten seconds.

That's exactly how long Laney had been in the truck, listening as Logan and Seth discussed possible suspects. Logan seemed to have a long list of people who might want revenge. Drug dealers. Petty criminals. A murderer who'd threatened to destroy Logan. A lawyer who'd been accused and convicted of peddling child pornography and told Logan that he'd make him pay. They all had motive. The problem was, they were all still in jail.

Or so Logan said as he tapped his hand on his thigh.

The same hand Laney had been holding.

She frowned, swiping her palm across her jeans, her hand still tingling from the warmth of his touch.

"You okay?" Logan asked, his attention shifting to her.

"You didn't mention Mildred," she responded, not wanting to discuss how she was doing. "She's not in jail."

"She's another possibility. I just figured I'd discuss that with Seth later."

"When I wasn't around to hear it? I'm not that fragile." But she did have a lump in her throat because the thought of her mother going to such lengths to hurt him made her physically ill.

"Who's Mildred?" Seth asked.

"My mother." If she could be called that, and Laney didn't think she could.

"Explain," he said, and Logan filled him in, giving a brief rundown, probably trying to spare Laney's feelings.

He didn't realize that anything and everything she'd felt for her parents had ceased to matter a long time ago.

She shifted, turning her attention to the blackness outside the window. They'd driven more than a hundred and fifty miles, and signs for Seattle dotted the side of the road. Another fifty and she'd be almost home. Only it wasn't really home. Not the kind she'd always wanted. One with a husband, kids, a family circle that she would always and forever be a part of.

Funny how that dream had never died.

"Sounds like we need to pay Mildred a visit." Seth turned onto a narrow dirt road. "Anyone know where she is?"

"Not yet, but we should be able to find out easily enough," Logan responded. Laney could feel that he was watching her.

She didn't turn to meet his eyes, just leaned her head back and closed her eyes, letting the two men talk because her cheek and jaw hurt, her head ached and every time she thought about her parents, her heart ached, too.

They'd taken a family legacy and destroyed it. Nearly destroyed her, too. If she ever went back to Green Bluff, she'd have to rebuild what her great-great grandfather had worked so hard to achieve. Not just a beautiful home on a beautiful piece of property, but a family of integrity, honor and faith.

She could almost picture it—the old house gleaming, the porch whitewashed and shimmering in the sunlight, laughter spilling out of open windows, children running through the orchards pulling ripe apples from the trees.

"We're here." Logan pulled her from the edge of dreams, and she fumbled for the door handle, then tumbled out into crisp cold air.

Here was a small ranch-style home at the end of a cul-de-sac. Four other houses stood sentinel nearby, each on a small lot. It was in a tidy neighborhood in the suburbs of Seattle. The perfect place to hide?

Maybe, but it wasn't what Laney had been expecting.

She'd thought they'd be in the middle of nowhere, next to nothing in a house surrounded by high fences and guarded by vicious dogs.

She followed Logan and Seth around the side of the house and in through a back door. Lights were on in the small kitchen, and a pretty blonde woman sat at a table there, her eyes on a computer monitor.

"You guys are running late." She smiled but didn't look away from the monitor.

"We took the long way." Seth shrugged out of his coat and took a seat beside her. "How are we looking?"

"Everything is online, and we're hooked into the security system."

"You sticking around or heading out?" Seth asked the woman.

"Sticking around."

"You know this case is trouble, right?" Seth pressed.

"That's what makes it fun." She grinned. "Laney, I have a room set up for you at the end of the hall. We'll be bunking together when I'm not pulling shift. I'm Taryn, by the way." She had pretty blue eyes, a stunning face and a soft smile, but her handshake was firm, her palm calloused.

"Nice to meet you."

"Because Seth is too boneheaded to tell you what's going on, I'll fill you in. We've been contracted by Personal Securities Incorporated to provide protection for you and Logan."

"Contracted by whom?"

"Ourselves. Darius said you needed some help. Seth and I had some time on our hands."

"Speak for yourself, blondie. I've got a full schedule." Seth turned the computer monitor and stared at the screen, his thick brows pulled together over ocean-blue eyes. A dark purple scar ran from the corner of his mouth to his temple. Another snaked up his neck. He looked tough and a little terrifying.

Actually, *a lot* terrifying.

"I owe you both." Logan dropped his coat on a chair. He was shorter than Seth and not nearly as broad, his muscles lean rather than bulky. But his presence was undeniable, his energy sweeping into the room and filling every corner of it.

Irresistible, and they'd be living in the same house until Logan's name could be cleared and the men who'd framed him had been thrown in jail. Maybe she could expedite things, do a little online research and try to help find Mildred.

"Do you have a computer? I'd like to—"

"No email. No contact with the outside world," Seth growled.

"I thought I'd do some online research and see if I can find out where my mother is."

"We'll take care of that," Seth responded, not even bothering to look away from the computer.

"I'd really like to help."

"The best thing you can do is put some ice on those bruises and get some rest." Logan opened the freezer, dropped several ice cubes into a paper towel and pressed it to her cheek, his fingers grazing her skin, the touch so light she barely felt it.

She wanted to lean in, press closer.

But she brushed his hands away and held the ice herself. "So, you're telling me that while all the capable people work to solve our problem, I should catch a few hours of sleep?"

"It's *my* problem. *Only* my problem. The fact that you're involved is pure chance." Logan took her arm and pulled her into a wide hall. Several doors opened from it, the rooms beyond dark, the wood floor dust coated and dull. The setup seemed rushed, as if the house had been closed for a long time and opened suddenly.

"There is no such thing as pure chance, Logan. Isn't that what you told me when you handed me the money and said I should leave Green Bluff? *Nothing happens by chance. I was put in your life for a reason. This is it*."

"That was a long time ago." He opened the door at the end of the hall and flicked on the light. The room, small with twin beds and a tall dresser, looked lived in and old. One small window looked out over the backyard.

"Time doesn't change truth. What you said made sense then, and it still does. God brought you into my life when I needed you, and he has brought me into yours now that you need me."

"This isn't about what anyone needs, Laney. It's about staying one step ahead of some very dangerous people."

"I can help you do that. If my mother does want to reconnect with me, we'll set it up. I'll pick her brain, see if I can find out how she feels about you."

"Too dangerous."

"Says who?"

"Me."

"I'm the best person to contact my mother. We both know it. If she's really hoping to get back into the house and back into Green Bluff's good graces, I'm her way to do it."

Logan frowned and ran a hand down his jaw. "I don't like it."

"But you know that I'm right."

"I'm a lot of things, Laney, but I'm not a fool. We have one shot at getting what we want from your mother. I'm not willing to waste it on something that might not work out."

"Exactly."

"There's one thing, though." He touched her cheek. "You

were attacked, beaten black and blue. I wasn't asking you to ice your cheek and lie down because I think you're weaker or less capable then the rest of us. I was asking you to because you look done in and I'm worried about you." He pressed a kiss to her forehead and walked out of the room, leaving her standing with her mouth open and her pulse racing.

He'd disarmed her, and she felt raw and open.

She didn't like the feeling.

Not at all.

She closed the door, her heart beating too rapidly, her thoughts scattered and unclear. She'd had big plans to start fresh, but she'd never imagined her new beginning would bring her back to the life she'd run from so many years ago. She'd never imagined that she'd see Logan again, and she'd never imagined that she might consider keeping the family home.

Never imagined that she'd meet with her mother.

That she'd *want* to meet with her.

Mildred. Mom. Whatever name Laney used for her, she was the same. A memory that Laney mostly wanted to forget. One of the worst parts of her childhood. Vindictive and mean, a consummate liar. A woman who was ruled by greed and bitterness.

Laney had promised herself she would never be that. She'd tried to so hard to stay focused on the positive and to conduct herself in a way that others would view as above reproach.

If anyone had asked her a week ago, she would have said that there was no way she'd ever be running from the police. That there was no way she'd need bodyguards. Her life had been secure and stable, even a little predictable, and that had been the way she'd wanted it.

She dropped onto the twin bed closest to the door, pressing the ice to her throbbing cheek. Her duffel was in the kitchen, and she didn't plan to retrieve it. She didn't want to face Logan again and feel the thrum of awareness as she looked in his eyes.

Her past.

That was all, but he seemed like so much more than that.

Nothing happened by chance.

She'd thrown those words at Logan, and she believed them. A reason for everything. She just didn't know what the reason for *this* was. Two weeks to clean up the remnants of her life and move on. Instead, she'd found herself steeped in the past, forced to face everything that had been.

Someone knocked on the door, and Laney sat up. "Come in."

Logan walked in, the duffel in one hand, a plastic bag full of ice in the other. "I brought you some fresh ice and your things."

"Thanks." She shoved the dripping paper towel into the bag and held it against her cheek. Her chest felt tight and her throat clogged. She'd loved Logan so much when they were kids. He'd been the big brother she'd never had. Her protector. Her friend. Her hero.

"We found Mildred." He settled on the edge of the bed, his hip close to hers. He'd sat the same way dozens of times when they were kids. It felt different now. More intimate.

"That was fast."

"She remarried a few years ago. Her engagement announcement popped up in an online newspaper. Once we knew her new name, it was easy enough to find her." He lifted the end of her ponytail, letting it slide through his fingers.

"What now?"

"We thought about having you call her to set up a meeting."

"I can do that." Although the thought chilled her to the bone.

"I know, but it might be best if you just show up. That will throw Mildred off balance and give you the advantage."

"That'll work, too."

"Her place isn't far from here. We'll leave early in the morning. Make sure that we get there before she has a chance to leave for the day."

She nodded, but she couldn't speak, the thought of facing Mildred stealing every word.

"Scared?" He touched her shoulder, his hand resting there for a moment.

"Yes."

"Don't be, Laney. She can't hurt you anymore."

"I'm not worried about her hurting me."

"Then what are you worried about?"

"That I'll still be as desperate for her affection as I was when I was a kid. That I'll let myself believe the lies she's going to tell."

"You're too strong to let that happen."

"I don't feel strong."

"That's because you're tired. Get some sleep, okay? We'll be leaving pretty early in the morning." The mattress shifted as he stood, the air around Laney suddenly cooler.

She didn't call him back as he walked out the door.

But she wanted to.

THIRTEEN

"Are you sure she lives here?" Laney asked as Taryn parked in front of a tiny bungalow sandwiched between two run-down Victorians.

She sounded doubtful.

Logan felt the same way.

He leaned past her and stared at the unassuming house.

It was not a place that either of them would have expected to find Mildred Mackey. She'd always been into opulent, showy things. Money had been her addiction, and she'd craved it like other people craved alcohol. When Logan had heard that she'd remarried, he'd assumed that she'd married money and was living in a grand house in an upscale neighborhood.

The little bungalow was anything but that.

"It looks as if the mighty have fallen pretty far," Taryn said, a hint of amusement in her voice. Aside from the gun she'd concealed under her coat, she could have been anyone, with her hair pulled into a ponytail and a perpetual smile on her face. A purplish scar peeked out from beneath a heavy fall of bangs—the only sign of the dangerous life she lived.

"She must have been in even more desperate straits before if this is what she married into. Are you ready, Laney?" Logan asked. She'd spent the twenty-minute ride in silence, her muscles so taut he'd wanted to knead the tension from them. He hadn't.

"I think so." She stared out the window and seemed as reluctant to look in his eyes as he was to touch her.

Kissing her had been a big mistake, but he couldn't afford to let it muddle either of their thinking. Not when there was so much at stake. He wouldn't allow himself to be distracted.

Even if he *could* smell strawberries and sunshine in Laney's hair every time he got close.

"If you don't want to do this—" he said.

"I want to. I'm just not sure that I'm *ready* to."

"You're going to be fine." He touched her arm, and she finally met his eyes. Fear. Determination. He saw them both in the depth of her gaze.

"Here's how this is going to play out," Seth grumbled. "Taryn will escort Laney to the house. Logan and I will stay here."

"I don't like that plan." Not when Laney looked terrified, and not when he wasn't sure what she'd find in the tiny house. Had Mildred changed? Or was she the same sadistic abuser she'd been thirteen years ago?

He didn't even need to ask.

A tiger didn't change its stripes.

"Tough." Seth's gaze was on the house, and Logan didn't think he expected to be argued with. He seemed like the kind of guy used to calling the shots.

So was Logan.

That might be a problem.

"Says who?" As far as Logan recalled, they'd never discussed the plan, and he wasn't going to walk blindly into it because Seth said he should.

"Me."

"Now that you've had your say, I'm going to explain the

way that *I* think things should go. You escort the ladies inside—"

"I'm surprised, Logan. I didn't take you for one of those he-man types who believe that a man can do a better professional security job than a woman," Taryn interrupted, still smiling. Logan didn't miss the sharp edge in her gaze.

"I'm not, but Laney and Mildred have a history, and it's not a good one. She may need a little extra support during the meeting."

"*She* is sitting right beside you, and *she'll* be just fine." Laney sounded confident, but her muscles were tense, her eyes rimmed with dark shadows, her face pale. The bruises stood out in stark contrast. Logan didn't want her to go in the house at all. That was the problem.

"Come on. We're wasting time. Let's get in there." Taryn jumped out of the truck and opened Laney's door.

"Right," Laney muttered, but as she got out, she didn't even shoot Logan a second glance.

Good, because if he saw fear in her eyes, he'd probably follow her.

And that wasn't a good idea.

As much as he wanted to protect Laney, he couldn't risk letting Mildred know that he was with her. The woman would be on the phone and calling the police before they even had a chance to find out what she'd spent the past couple of years doing.

Laney closed the door, and he watched as she made her way across the small yard. Taryn walked beside her, at ease but on alert, her hand beneath her coat, ready to pull out her firearm if necessary.

"Glad you're using your brain on this one, deputy," Seth said, his gaze shifting to Logan, his eyes a strange color between blue and green and devoid of emotion.

"I usually do."

"Not when it comes to Laney."

"Maybe not."

"No maybes about it. You shouldn't be here at all. You should have stayed back at the safe house like I told you to."

True. Logan wouldn't deny it.

"Unfortunately, I'm here, so discussing what I should have done seems like a waste of time," he pointed out.

"What I have to say next isn't."

"Spit it out then."

"Letting yourself be influenced by emotions is never a good thing. If you don't watch it, you're going to get all of us thrown into jail."

"I suppose you would have handled things differently?" Logan asked because he figured that Seth was the kind of guy who had an answer for everything and played every game by the book.

"I'd like to think that I would have. Hard to tell, though. If my girlfriend were heading into trouble, I'd probably insist on being with her. No matter what."

"Laney isn't my girlfriend."

"Could have fooled me." Seth turned his attention back to the house.

"She's an old friend. Someone tried to kill her because of me. That changed the rules I'm playing by."

"Hmph" was Seth's only response.

Logan let it lie, watching as the bungalow's door opened.

He caught a glimpse of blond hair and a thin frame, a pretty face perfectly made up.

Mildred.

Seeing her infuriated him. She should still be in jail, serving time for the crimes that she'd committed.

"That looks like our mark," Seth muttered.

"It is."

"She's aged well."

"She's only forty-eight."

"She had Laney young."

"When she was nineteen. She wasn't able to conceive again after that." At least, that was the story. Whether or not it was the truth was something that Logan had never been able to figure out.

"Maybe that's why she was such a terrible parent—she wanted more children, and she was bitter from too many disappointments."

"You've got a good imagination, Sinclair, but I'm sure that she wasn't disappointed about not having more children. Laney was her little doll. She dressed her up, brought her out for visitors to see, stuck her back in her room until the next special occasion and beat her while they waited for it."

"Nice."

"Yeah. The woman is mean to the bone."

"Still?"

"I don't know."

"She must be if she's responsible for the attempt on your life. Anyone who'd go to the kind of efforts that she has to ruin someone's name knows exactly how to carry a grudge and keep it."

"We haven't proven that she's responsible."

"We will." Seth sounded confident. Logan wanted to feel the same. After nearly eight months of telling everyone who'd listen that he was innocent, he'd love to be able to prove it. He'd love to go back to his town, his house, his life. More than that, he'd like to know that he hadn't dragged three other people into the nightmare that he'd been living through.

"If not, I'm not the only one who's going to be in trouble."

"No need to remind me of the risk, Randal. I know what we're playing for." Seth shifted in his seat, took binoculars from the glove compartment and aimed them at the bungalow's front window. "Can't see a thing."

"Mind if I look?"

"Go ahead." Seth handed him the binoculars. "Bet you wish you could be in there trying to get a read on Mildred. It's what I'd want to do."

"Yeah."

"So maybe we give the ladies a few minutes to feel things out and then we head inside. It's not like the police don't know you and Laney are together, right?"

"They're probably assuming that we are."

"No probably about it. Ronald Danvers has been talking nonstop since he was brought in for questioning. He told the authorities all about how you knocked him down, tied him up and ran off with his good friend Laney."

"You heard this where?" Logan lowered the binoculars, leaning over the front seat so he could look into Seth's face. His expression showed nothing, though Logan thought there might be a hint of excitement in the depth of his eyes.

"Darius. I spoke to him this morning while you and the rest of our quartet were sleeping." Seth grinned. "He knows the local sheriff, and he called the guy and asked what was going on out at the Mackey place last night. The whole town is buzzing about it, so it's not like it's a secret."

"And?"

"The police in Green Bluff aren't stupid, but you know that. You worked for them for years."

He had, and he knew that if there'd been any evidence at all to support Logan's claim of innocence, his coworkers would have been all over it. "They're a good team."

"Yeah, and none of them are buying what Roland is selling. A guy named Tanner told Darius that Roland is dirt, and that he doesn't believe a word of his story. Says the guy has a record a mile long and three warrants out for his arrest."

"That doesn't surprise me. Did Tanner mention anything about the Cascade Mountain Men?"

"Yes. His office is checking into the connection. We should probably do the same."

"I agree." Logan figured the more they knew about it, the better.

"Do you also agree that we've left Laney and Taryn in there long enough?" Seth said.

"Absolutely."

"Then let's go see what Mildred has to say for herself." Seth jumped out of the truck.

Logan followed, his nerves humming with adrenaline as he walked to the house. It had been ten years since he'd faced Mildred in court. She'd given a convincing testimony, but there'd been too much stacked against her. Kids who she'd slapped, starved, demeaned. Adults who'd been troubled teens hoping for a fresh start and who'd gotten nothing but hatred.

She'd stared Logan down during her sentencing, and he'd seen something in her eyes that might have worried him if she hadn't been wearing prison orange and handcuffs.

Maybe it *should* have worried him.

She was spiteful, vindictive and smart. That could be a deadly combination.

"Let's go around back first. I want to see what our escape options are if the police show while we're in there." Logan didn't wait for Seth's response, just headed around the side of the little house, the gun holster that Seth had lent him a comforting weight against his chest.

Armed. Ready. Just the way he had been hundreds of times when he'd worked as a police officer. He wanted to go back to that life so badly, he could taste it.

A step at a time, he'd get there.

He had to believe it. He had to trust that God had a plan, and that plan didn't include Logan rotting in prison for the rest of his life.

FOURTEEN

"Are you sure that you don't want tea?" Mildred asked for the seventeenth time, and Laney had to bite back a sharp retort. Letting her anger show wouldn't loosen her mother's tongue, and that's the only thing she cared about.

Not the mean little room where they sat with Mildred's ancient husband, every inch of it pristine. Not the strands of white that threaded through Mildred's once perfectly colored hair.

Not the greedy, hungry look in Mildred's eyes.

Laney shuddered, looking down at her shoes and wishing herself far away from the house and its occupants.

"No tea, Mother. And if you don't have any information that will help, then Taryn and I need to get out of here."

"But you've only been here a few minutes, and I was hoping we could catch up."

"On what?" she asked bluntly, not caring that the words were cold and hard.

"Your life."

"Why?"

"Because you came to see me."

"Not because I wanted to."

"Of course you wanted to. No one held a gun to your head and demanded that you visit me. No matter what happened in the past, there's a bond between mother and daughter that can't be broken. *That's* why you're here, whether you realize it or not." For the first time since Mildred had opened the door, she sounded like the woman Lacey had grown up with—manipulative and determined to have her way.

"You're wrong. I'm not interested in some imaginary bond, and I'm not interested in catching up. I'm interested in finding Logan Randal. Has he contacted you?" She stuck to the script that Logan had rehearsed with her on the drive from the safe house, and Mildred frowned.

"No. I told you that already. And really, Laney, I don't know why you'd want to find him."

"Because he's in trouble and I want to help him."

"According to the news, you already have. As a matter of fact, the last I heard, the police were looking for you. They're saying that the two of you are together. Obviously, that's not the case."

"We were together. Logan saved my life last night, then he dropped me off at a friend's house and left." The rehearsed script again, and she was sure there was disappointment in Mildred's eyes.

"They're offering a big reward for information that leads to his capture. Did you know that?"

"No." But hearing it made Laney's heart skip a beat.

"Twenty-thousand dollars. That would go a long way to fund the orphanage Stan and I are building in Mexico. Wouldn't it, dear?" She smiled lovingly at the white-haired man who sat beside her, and ice ran through Laney's blood.

She knew that smile, knew the hatred it hid.

Whatever Mildred's reason for marrying, it hadn't been love.

"That's right, dear, but we must remember that the young man's soul is important, too. We should be praying for him rather than hoping to profit from his capture." Stan's eyes were rheumy, his hands splotched with age marks, but there was something in his gaze when he looked at Laney that unsettled her. A directness, a sharpness that seemed at odds with his slumped shoulders and frail appearance.

"Of course. You're so much better a person than I am." Mildred patted his age-marked hand, and Laney was sure that Stan winced.

Was Mildred abusing the poor old guy? He looked to be at least eighty. She wanted to put her arm around his frail shoulders and tell him to run as fast as his legs would carry him.

"Since you don't want any tea, dear, how about some breakfast? I can make omelets and toast. You can tell me about your career. The private eye that I hired a few years ago said that you graduated college and were an interior designer. I'm so proud of you." Mildred's gaze settled on Laney; she had that predatory look in her eyes, both hungry and terrifying.

"If you're hoping that pretending to be a good mother will put you back in my good graces, your hopes are going to be in vain." Laney bit the words out, and Taryn gave a subtle shake of the head.

Stick to the script, Laney could almost hear her say.

She didn't want to, though.

Her mother hadn't changed. She was the same grasping, clawing abuser that she'd been when Laney was young.

"Pretend to be a good mother? I *was* a good mother. An excellent one." Mildred huffed.

"Now, dear, don't get yourself riled up. Perhaps some of the medicine the doctor prescribed…" Stan started, and Mildred rounded on him, her eyes blazing.

"Listen, you old—"

Whatever she'd planned to say was lost as the front door flew open and crashed into the wall.

Mildred screamed and poor old Stan nearly fell off the couch. Laney jumped in front of him, terrified that a stray bullet would end the old man's life and that it would be her fault for being in his house. Only Taryn seemed unfazed. She pulled her gun, then aimed it, but her expression never changed.

"Hold your fire." Seth stepped into the house with Logan right behind him. The door closed solidly, the sharp bang breaking the sudden silence.

"You're lucky that I didn't already pull the trigger. We follow the plan, remember? And this wasn't part of it." Taryn's sharp tone matched the hardness in her face. She tucked the gun back into its holster, her smile gone. For the first time since Laney had met her, she looked like what she was.

"You're too good at what you do to pull the trigger before you know who's on the barrel end of it." Seth's nonchalant attitude made Taryn frown, but any response she might have made was cut off by Mildred's shriek.

"Logan Randal! In my house! Call the police, Stan! Now!" She ran at Logan, and Seth pulled her up short, barely avoiding her clawed hand.

"Cool it, lady."

"Cool it! The man is a criminal. Do you know that?"

"I'm not the only one who has served time, Mildred," Logan said coolly, his jacket pulled back just enough for Laney to glimpse the handgun strapped to his chest. It was William's, but Laney's life with her husband seemed so far away it could have been a dream, her love for William muted colors compared to the vividness of Logan's presence in her life.

"You're the only one who is an escaped felon. The only one who is wanted by the police!" Mildred spat, the hatred in her eyes and in her voice so thick, Laney was surprised that she didn't choke on it.

This was Mildred at her finest.

The Mildred of Laney's childhood nightmares, only

smaller and diminished by time, her power stolen by all the years they'd spent apart. She could spew all she wanted, but she couldn't hurt Laney anymore. She wouldn't hurt Logan either.

"Logan isn't a criminal, Mother," Laney said, knowing that she'd draw her mother's attention and her wrath.

"Shut up, you little witch." Mildred turned on her, the sweet-natured facade that she'd been wearing since Laney entered the house stripped away.

"I'm not a kid anymore. I can speak when I want to."

"And say what? The same thing you spent every day of your teenage years saying?"

"What's that supposed to mean?" Laney hadn't said much to her mother, not when she was child or a teen, but she was curious to know how the past had been twisted to fit Mildred's lies.

"You and Logan were always plotting against me, making up stories, trying to convince the world that I was a monster." Mildred scowled, jabbing a finger in Logan's direction. "He's a bad apple, Laney. He always has been. He came into our lives, and he destroyed our family. I can't believe you would even defend him."

"He didn't beat the tar out of me every other day for sixteen years, Mildred. I guess that's a good enough reason to defend him."

"Why, you ungrateful little—"

"I think we're done here." Logan grabbed Laney's hand and pulled her to the door. Too bad, because she had more to say to her mother. A lot more. Years of words she'd tucked down deep because she'd been too afraid to speak them.

"So that's what this is about. You're a couple." Mildred's brittle laughter filled the room, the caustic sound enough to chill Laney's blood. Whatever her mother's problems, they hadn't gotten better over time.

Poor Stan.

He'd bear the brunt of it when they left.

He stood a few feet away. No phone in his hand. If he'd called the police, Laney hadn't heard him.

She met his eyes. "I'm sorry, Stan."

"For?"

"Disturbing your life. If there's ever anything I can do—"

"Shut up!" Mildred snapped. "Both of you, or I'll make you sorry that you didn't."

"You don't have that kind of control over me anymore, Mother. And if I find out that you're the one who set Logan up—" Laney pushed for what they'd come for, hoping and praying that they'd get it before they walked out the door.

"He set himself up. He went down the wrong path, and now he's paying for it. That's the way life is. Look at what happened to your father and me."

"Mother—"

"Don't feel sorry for me. I don't want it, and I don't need it. I had a great life until Logan walked into it—"

"I didn't walk. You dragged me. I was a fourteen-year-old kid, and it's not like I had any choice," Logan cut in, ready and willing to take control of the conversation.

"You had a choice not to be such a little hooligan."

"You seem awfully angry, Mildred. I suppose that comes from having someone ruin your life." He threw it out there and wondered if she'd bite.

"You're right. It does. You stole my life and my marriage. You took everything and left me with nothing. The happiest day of my life was when I heard that you'd be spending your life in jail. Just deserts. That's what I said. Didn't I, Stan?"

"You did." The elderly man, who'd been leaning against the wall and watching, spoke. Despite his obvious age, he carried himself like a military man, his sharp gray gaze settling on Logan.

"I'm Stan Dubois. Mildred's husband. I've heard a lot about you, Logan."

"I'm sure that you have." Logan took his proffered hand, surprised at the strength behind Stan's handshake. The guy had to be eighty, a few decades older than his wife.

"Nonstop for the past couple of years," Stan responded. "You're not what I pictured."

"Is that a compliment or an insult?" Logan asked as Seth walked to the front window and looked out into the early-morning sunlight.

"Just an observation. I used to be a military man, you know. After that, I worked for the Seattle Police Department for thirty years."

Uh oh. Not good.

"I think it's time to hit the road," Seth said before Logan could.

"I think you're right. Let's go." Logan flung open the door and hurried Laney to the truck.

Mildred didn't bother following. No doubt she was already on the phone with the police.

"A retired cop. What are the odds?" Taryn muttered as she slid behind the wheel.

"Hold on there!" Stan called.

"I don't think so." Taryn turned the key in the ignition and fired up the engine. It would have been easy enough to drive away and leave the old guy in their dust, but Logan saw something in his eyes and in his tone that made him hesitate.

He put his hand on Taryn's shoulder. "Let's hear what he has to say."

"I don't like it, but because you're the one who has the most to lose if we're caught, I guess we can go with your plan."

"Just watch out. The guy is probably packing heat. For all we know, he's going to pull a gun and demand we get out and wait for his backup to arrive." Seth didn't seem happy about the delay, but Logan didn't care.

He had a feeling about Stan. The guy was closer to Mildred than anyone else. If she was hiding something, if she was somehow connected to the plot against him, Stan was the one who'd know it.

Whether he'd be willing to share, that was another thing altogether.

FIFTEEN

One minute they were making their escape, and the next Stan Dubois was climbing into the truck, scooting in next to Laney. She had no choice but to move to the center of the seat, her shoulder wedged firmly against Logan's.

She tried not to notice how warm Logan was and how firm his biceps felt. She tried not to notice the way her heart slammed against her ribs at the contact.

"I thought you had some common sense in you. I see that I was right." Stan slammed the door. "Better get going. Mildred is already on the phone, and it won't take long for Seattle P.D. to dispatch officers to the area."

"You can't come with us, Mr. Dubois," Taryn said calmly, but her knuckles were white, her hands gripping the steering wheel so hard Laney thought she heard the leather crackle.

"I'm not sure that you're right about that, young lady."

"I'm not that young, and I'm the one driving, so I guess it's my decision to make."

"You have a point, but because I'm not getting out of the truck, I'd say that I have the upper hand," Stan pointed out.

"I can remove you from the car, old man," Seth growled, and Stan smiled.

"And waste time that would be better spent making your escape? I don't think any of you are that stupid."

"What do you want, Dubois?" Logan asked, leaning around Laney to eye the older man. His hair brushed her chin, and his hand brushed her thigh. She stilled, almost afraid to breathe for fear that she would inhale his scent and be carried away by it.

"To help."

"Why?"

"Because I believe in justice. I didn't think you got it at your trial, and I don't think you're going to get it now. Plus, I'm bored out of my mind and raring for some action," he responded matter-of-factly, his gaze jumping to the house and to Mildred. She stood in the door, a phone pressed to her ear. "Now, I really do think we'd better go because Mildred doesn't feel quite the same way about the situation as I do."

Taryn muttered something under her breath and pulled away from the house.

Stan seemed content to lean back in his seat and watch the scenery flash by. Short of pulling over and forcefully removing him, there didn't seem to be much that they could do about it.

"Turn left at the next crossroad," he said, and Logan frowned.

"You may be catching a ride, but you're not calling the shots."

"Mildred doesn't have the brains to set you up, Logan, but I think I know who does. I thought we could pay his office a visit and see if we can find what we need to prove it. Of course, if you'd rather not, we can just keep heading wherever you're going and forget the little side trip I have planned."

"What are you talking about?" Logan pressed in even closer, leaning past Laney to look in Stan's face. Laney felt every muscle, every hollow, every bit of his lean body. She wanted to move away, but there was nowhere to go. Nothing to do but wait things out and pray that when this was over, she'd be able to forget the way it felt to have him so close.

"Mildred had a son before she married Josiah Mackey."

"That's impossible. My parents grew up together. They were good friends before they started dating, and they married as soon as my father graduated from college," Laney cut in, her voice too high and her stomach churning. She'd heard the story a million times from a million people growing up. She'd been the only child of the golden family, the one charged with keeping the Mackey family name alive. The weight of her heritage had rested on her shoulders. A day hadn't gone by when her father and mother hadn't reminded her of the fact.

"It's very possible. Not that Mildred shared the information with me," Stan said. "She preferred that I think of her as a wrongly accused woman whose husband had subjected her to such abuse that she'd done whatever he'd wanted. After we married, when my head was screwed on a little tighter, I started noticing all the holes in Mildred's story."

"It doesn't sound like you're very fond of her. Considering that you two are married, that's surprising," Seth cut in. Stan shrugged.

"Not every marriage is a happy one, is it? The fact is, I met Mildred during the lowest point of my life. My wife of forty years had just passed away, and there was a huge hole I was desperate to fill. Mildred walked into church one Sunday, and I was taken in by her smile and charm. It took me a little too long to realize it was all an act."

"You mentioned her taking some medicine when we were in the house. Do you really think that will help someone like her?" Laney asked, not sure what good medicine would do for the kind of soul sickness that Mildred had.

"She's on antianxiety medication. The time she spent in prison did a number on her nerves."

"I don't think it was her time in prison that did that," Laney muttered. Mildred had always been moody and anxious, but that wasn't what they should be discussing. "You said that she had a son before she had me."

"That's right. I did a little investigating after we were married. She was too secretive for my liking, and I couldn't live with that. Plus, she'd taken a substantial amount of money from our account, and she wasn't forthcoming about what she'd used it for. Handbags, shoes and cosmetics, she'd said."

"Actually, Mildred always loved those things. I can imagine her spending a lot of money on them." She'd always had the best of everything, and she'd always wanted more.

"True, but there was something not right about her story. I dug around and found out that she'd hired a P.I. to find you and a man who was a few years older. I had a little talk with the P.I., and he was happy to explain things."

"Not into client confidentiality, huh?" Logan cut in.

"For the right price, most people will talk."

"Want to tell us what he said before I dump you out on the side of the road for talking too much?" Seth muttered, but the energy in the truck had shifted. Everyone was focused on Stan and whatever information he was about to share.

"Mildred had Chris when she was seventeen. Her parents farmed her out to one of those homes for unwed mothers, and she gave him up after he was born. Apparently, his father was a member of her church, a wealthy older gentleman who was already married. I'd like to say that she was naive, but I don't think Mildred has ever been that. More than likely, she thought he'd leave his wife, marry her and give her the life she always thought she deserved."

"That sounds like Mildred. Manipulative. Conniving. Spiteful." Logan's hand drifted along Laney's arm and wove its way beneath the heavy fall of her hair.

He kneaded the tense muscles in her neck, the gesture so

natural and easy that she couldn't deny it any more than she could deny the way her muscles went liquidy and soft at his touch.

"True," Stan continued. "But I still don't think she has the brains to set up the kind of sting that took you down. She'd have had to know a lot about the way the law works. She'd have had to know the inner workings of the police department. She's more the kind of woman who knows how to jerk the emotions. I don't think she could have created this kind of trouble."

"I'm not so sure about that." Logan's hand dropped away, leaving cold where warmth had been.

Laney shouldn't care. Should not have wanted to move in close and gather up more of what he'd offered, but she did. She held herself stiff and tried to concentrate on Stan. "I am. Mother has always taken the easy route. If she wanted you punished, she'd have found someone who could make sure it happened, and she'd have let him or her take care of it for her."

"Exactly!" Stan beamed at her as if she'd just proved herself his star pupil, and Laney couldn't help smiling as she looked into his sparkling gray eyes.

"She tried to use you, didn't she?" Taryn asked.

"Well, she didn't marry me for my money or my looks, that's for sure. She spent the first couple years of our marriage moaning about the damage Logan had done to her. I finally told her that as a Christian woman, she needed to take the higher road and forgive. Next thing that I knew, money was missing from our account."

"Let me guess, she never mentioned Logan again after she found her son." Laney could picture Mildred, undaunted by Stan's refusal to help, determined to get her revenge at any cost.

"Right again. She must have thought she could gain the sympathy of either you or Chris. Obviously, you wanted nothing to do with her, having spent your childhood with her. Chris, though, was looking for what she offered."

"Family?" Laney thought that must be what most people wanted. Connection and love. A sense that they belonged with someone.

"Yes. His adoptive parents divorced when he was a kid, and his father had custody. His mother hadn't been a big part of his life, and Mildred used that to her advantage. Turn right at the light. We're going to the law offices of Banks and Brinkman. It's on the next—"

"Are you talking about Chris Banks?" Shocked, Laney forgot about what she shouldn't do and grabbed Logan's hand.

"Yes."

"He's my father's attorney. *My* attorney." Her stomach churned, her mind going a million miles an hour.

"I didn't know that, but it doesn't surprise me. Mildred received notice about your father's illness a few months before she hired the P.I. She probably thought that having Chris get in good with your father would open up a way for her to get back the land and the house that she felt Logan stole from her. She loved that place, and she always hoped that your father would decide to leave it to her. She wasn't happy when she learned that you were the one who'd inherited."

"I'm sure that she wasn't." Laney leaned her head against the seat.

Her head ached from too many sleepless nights, and her cheek and jaw throbbed from the beating she'd taken. Her heart hurt, too; her chest felt tight and heavy. She was drained. All her thoughts about closure and new beginnings seemed so far out of reach, she wasn't sure she'd ever be able to grasp them.

Logan squeezed her hand, his gentleness made tears burn behind her eyes. He was so much more than what William had been. Bigger than life. Demanding. Being with him would never be the safe thing to do. Not when it came to her heart.

"What are we thinking? Do I turn here? Or do we kick Stan out and go back to the safe house?" Taryn asked as she approached the turn.

"Might as well turn. Where to next, old man?" Seth asked, and Stan leaned forward.

"I may be old, but I can still take you down, kid. Keep that in mind when you're talking to me."

"Sorry, sir," Seth offered.

"Good. We're going to Chris's Seattle office. He's only there on Mondays and Fridays. We should be able to get in and out without a problem. No staff there on those days. Chris is frugal that way."

"You're suggesting that we break into his office?" Logan asked.

"I'm suggesting that if you want to find out who set you up, you should start with the most likely suspect and check out his associates. You were a police officer. You know that. The office is there on the corner. Pull around back. We can go in a service entrance."

"You realize that if we get caught, you're going to lose your marriage and your freedom, right?" Logan bit out.

"You realize that if we get caught, you might be up for the death penalty for killing the police officer who was escorting you to prison, right?"

"Not likely. The other officer lived. He knows I never fired a shot."

"Doesn't matter. If you're found responsible for hatching the escape plan, you'll be convicted of murder. That's a no-brainer, kid."

"You both realize that we're sitting in a parking lot wasting time, right?" Seth cut in.

"Good point. Let's get this show on the road." Stan sounded

excited at the prospect. The rest of the group didn't look quite as enthusiastic, but no one seemed to be able to argue the merit of his plan.

Seth got out of the truck and opened Stan's door. "This better not be a trap."

"How could it be? I didn't even know you were stopping by my house this morning."

"Maybe not, but you seem to know a lot of other things." Logan slid out of the truck, bright sunlight glinting in his hair.

Laney started to follow, but he shook his head.

"You stay here with Taryn. We'll be back as soon as we can."

"Not a good idea, deputy. They'll be sitting out here in the open, and your girlfriend's face has been all over the morning news. Someone is bound to see her and decide to call the cops. If that happens, we're all going down. She's coming with us." Seth pulled Laney from the truck, and she wasn't sure if she should be pleased or terrified. The other four members of their team were trained police officers or security experts. She was an interior designer. She was also a chicken. She hated scary movies and disliked surprises.

Safe and orderly.

That's how she wanted her life. It's what she'd craved as a kid and strived for as an adult.

She'd found it with William and had been trying to keep it after his death.

Now it was gone, and somehow she didn't think that she'd ever find it again.

SIXTEEN

The law offices of Banks and Brinkman were located on the top floor of the office building. Seven flights of stairs, and Laney felt every one. Not that she wasn't in decent shape, but the group was moving quickly and she was still sore. Even Stan. For a guy who looked like he was pushing eighty and who'd acted as fragile as old bone china when she'd met him, he could sure move fast.

She panted up the last flight of stairs, leaning against the wall as Seth and Logan scouted out the corridor beyond the stairwell.

"StairMaster, kid," Stan said with just a hint of breathlessness in his voice.

"What?"

"Get on the StairMaster a couple of times a day. By the time you're my age, seven flights of stairs will be a piece of cake." He grinned, his gray eyes sparkling with humor. How he'd ended up married to Mildred, Laney still couldn't understand. A black hole that sucked in emotion and energy and drained the people around her dry, she didn't seem like the kind of person someone like Stan would be attracted to. No matter how many empty holes he'd had that needed to be filled.

"Thanks for the advice. I'll take it into consideration." *If* she lived through the next few hours and days. The way things had been going, she wasn't sure that living was a certainty.

"No problem, but next time, I charge." He peered out the window in the stairwell door, looking into the corridor beyond. "Looks like one of our guys is coming back. Hopefully, we have a clear shot to Chris's office. I don't want to be stuck on the top floor of this building if the police come down on us. I'm not carrying firepower today." He sounded almost gleeful, and Taryn sighed.

"You sound just a little too happy about all this, Stan."

"In a few years, I may be pushing up daisies, so a little excitement in my life isn't a bad thing."

The door opened, and Seth peered in. "Hallway is clear. Looks like there are only two businesses up here. Both are closed for the day. There's a security camera near the elevator, but nothing near either door. We're good to go. Randal is accessing Banks's office."

To Laney that sounded an awful lot like he was breaking in.

Which, she supposed, was the point.

Breaking and entering. Harboring a felon. Aiding and abetting a criminal's escape.

Her life had definitely fallen into chaos. Unlike Stan, she wasn't exactly happy about it.

They rounded a corner and approached an open door.

Logan appeared in the doorway, his hair mussed and his jaw shadowed. He looked rugged, handsome and determined.

And he looked like home, like the best of what she'd had when she was growing up. Like every good memory, good feeling, good thought. Like exactly what she'd have wanted if she weren't so determined to go it alone.

"What are we looking for, chief?" Seth asked as they stepped into a posh waiting area. Black leather sofa and dark wood chairs. A glass coffee table with a vase of fresh flowers in its center. Artwork on the walls. *Real* art, not prints. Banks and Brinkman had spent a small fortune on wall decorations and furniture.

For such a young lawyer, Christopher was doing very well.

"We're looking for some connection to the guy who attacked Laney or to the militia group that sent him," Logan said. "I never had any dealing with the group, so they had no reason to have any with me. Someone else called the shots. I'm sure of it," Logan responded.

"You think that a guy who has all this would be stupid enough to leave a trail of evidence that connects him to a crime?" Taryn gestured around the office.

"I think that a guy who has all this might be just arrogant enough to think he's above suspicion," Logan responded.

"Why don't you take Laney and work Banks's office, deputy? Taryn and I will work Brinkman's. We'll leave Stan to work the reception area. Fifteen minutes, people. Then, we're out of here. Whether we've got something or not." Seth didn't wait to have his plan agreed on. He just walked to a door marked George Brinkman and went inside the room.

No problem. Logan was willing to go with the flow.

As long as he and Laney were paired together.

He'd gotten her into this mess.

He needed to make sure he got her out.

He pressed a hand to her back, urging her into a large corner office and ignoring the heat that shot through him at the contact.

"He's doing well for himself." Laney ran her hand over smooth mahogany, probably trailing a hundred fingerprints over the surface of the desk.

It didn't matter. Mildred had had plenty of time to tell the police that Laney and Logan were working together. Laney's fingerprints in Banks's office would be one small piece of the evidence that would be stacked against her if she was arrested and brought to trial.

"Very."

"If he's really Mildred's son, he's my half brother. That seems so…strange." She lifted a Rolodex from the desk and thumbed through it, her ponytail falling to the middle of her back. She looked young and vulnerable, the bruises on her skin a reminder of just how close she'd come to dying.

"Brother or not, he's going to have to pay if he hired Danvers to come after you."

"If he did that, then he did everything else, and he *should* pay for it. That's not why I was thinking about the family connection, though."

"No?" He opened a drawer, sifted through pens and paperclips and notepads. Nothing.

"If he and Mildred really did scheme to ruin your life, they're crazy. If they are—"

"Don't." He cut her off.

"What?"

"You are nothing like your mother, and you're nothing like Banks. You never have been. You never will be. End of story."

"Okay." She smiled, and his heart jumped. The yearning he felt for her was so intense that he had to look away.

A lifetime ago, Laney had been the sweet little girl he'd wanted desperately to protect. She'd been his reason for shaping up, towing the line. He'd wanted to be a better person for her, and that desire had made him into the man he'd become.

She wasn't a little girl anymore.

That much was for sure, and no matter how many times he'd tried to get her out of his life and to safety, she'd been thrust back into it.

God knew why. Logan was sure of that. He just wished that *he* did.

He yanked open another drawer.

"There's nothing in the Rolodex. Anything in the drawers?" She leaned close, strawberries and sunshine in her hair and mountain mist in her eyes, and if they'd been anywhere else, he might have leaned in to taste her lips.

He jerked his attention back to the drawer filled with boxes of cookies, packages of candy bars and rolls of antacids.

"Guy likes his snacks," he mumbled.

"This is like looking for a needle in a haystack—only even more impossible because we don't know what we're looking for." She smoothed her hair, her shirt sleeve riding up to reveal finger-sized bruises on her wrist.

"When we find it, we'll know."

"I hope you're right." She pulled a trash can out from under the desk, and he yanked at the third desk drawer.

Locked.

He took a paper clip from the drawer, unbent it and shoved it into the lock mechanism. He'd done this plenty when he'd been young and stupid. He'd hated the system that had taken him from the aging grandmother who'd been raising him while his father was in jail and his mother snorted coke. Grandma Sandy had been unable to curb his rebellious nature, but she'd loved him. When he'd been taken from her and thrown into a group home, he'd wanted to get at the system and at all the people who'd failed him. He'd found plenty of ways to do it.

He shoved the memories away, focusing on the lock and his improvised pick. It took longer than he would have liked, but he finally heard a quiet click. The drawer opened, and he smiled at what he found inside.

"What is it?" Laney asked.

"Files." He scanned the names but saw nothing that sparked his interest. "I don't know if they'll do us any good, though."

"This might." She handed him a piece of paper, crumbled

and ripped. Just a scrap really, with three letters scrawled across it. DAN. Big and bold.

"Is the rest of it in there?"

"I haven't been able to find it, but it's the first three letters of Danvers name. That seems pretty incriminating, don't you think?"

"It's circumstantial at best." But he had to admit it was intriguing.

"I'll keep looking." She dumped the contents of the trash can on the floor and started going through them.

He did the same with the files, lifting them out and carefully setting them on the desk. There had to be something else in the desk. In his time as a police officer, Logan had learned that the smartest criminals often made the biggest mistakes. Mostly because they thought they were too smart to get caught.

He ran his hands over the wood panel of the drawer, then yanked the entire thing off its tracks. He turned it over. Nothing. He crouched and peered into the cavity, smiling at the envelope taped to the wood, an 8 x 10 manila sealed with a piece of tape.

"What did you find?" Laney looked up from the pile of trash she was sorting through.

"I'm not sure." He slid his finger under the tape, pulled several pages from the envelope and saw his face staring out from a newspaper clipping.

"Seems Banks was interested in my arrest and trial." He glanced through the other pages. More of the same. Nothing to link Banks to Danvers, but it did show that he'd been interested in Logan. He'd had no reason to be. He wasn't a defense lawyer or a prosecutor.

"Why would he keep those clippings hidden?" Lacey's shoulder brushed his as she leaned to get a closer look. Her hair tickled his chin, the scent of strawberries drifting through the air.

She'd been so soft in his arms. So tempting.

"Good question." He replaced the drawer and the files and slid the pages back into the folder.

"It almost seems like he was fixated on you."

"Did you find anything else in the trash can?" He booted up Banks's computer.

"No. Just a few candy wrappers and a couple of crumbled-up papers that didn't say anything important." She put the trash can back under the desk.

"How about you go check the receptionist's desk and trash can? The rest of that page may be there."

"Shouldn't we be getting out of here?" She hesitated at the threshold of the room, twirling a strand of hair between her fingers.

"We have three minutes." And every one of them mattered. "Go check the other trash cans."

"Right." She pivoted and left the room.

Good. He needed to focus, and she was a distraction. More of one than he'd ever imagined sweet little Laney Mackey could be. When they were young, he'd never seen her as anything more than the little girl he had to protect. Even as she'd grown into a teenager, he'd only noticed in a perfunctory way. Little Laney. That's how he'd always thought of her.

He didn't seem to be thinking of her that way anymore.

He wasn't sure how he felt about that.

Numb maybe, but that's the way he'd been feeling about most things since Amanda's death. His arrest and incarceration hadn't changed it. As a matter of fact, there'd been a part of him that had almost felt as if he'd deserved the trouble he'd found himself in. Going on with his life, living while Amanda was dead—it had seemed inconceivable and somehow wrong.

It had taken him a year to work through that.

He didn't want to go there again. He didn't want to be sitting in jail picturing Laney doing the same. And not just

Laney. Three other people also would go down if they got caught in Banks's office.

He rifled through the desk drawers, found a letter opener and used it to unscrew the back off of the computer's hard drive. There wasn't time to try to guess Banks's password, but there was plenty of time to remove the computer's memory card.

"We're out of time," Taryn called from the doorway, and Logan shoved the memory card into his pocket and screwed the hard drive cover back into place.

There'd be something on the memory card.

There had to be.

SEVENTEEN

"Time to get out of here, kid." Stan tapped Laney's shoulder, and she looked up from the pile of trash she'd dumped on the floor. She didn't want to stop searching through the junk. Doing so felt too much like giving up.

All she needed was to find Danvers's name on a document with the office's letterhead. If she could find that, she was sure the police would listen. Unfortunately, she kept coming up empty. As far as she could tell, they'd searched the place for fifteen minutes and found nothing that would help prove Logan's innocence.

"I guess this was a waste of time."

"I wouldn't say that." Seth walked out of Brinkman's office, a file folder in his hand.

"What'd you find, rookie?" Stan asked, and Seth scowled.

"There'll be time to discuss it after we get out of here," Logan said, grabbing Laney's hand and pulling her to the door.

"I can't leave a pile of trash on the floor. Even if the office is closed for the day, a cleaning crew might come in and get suspicious."

"Taryn and I will take care of it. You get out of here." Logan nudged her into the hall.

"But—"

"Seth, you want to get Stan and Laney moving?"

"No problem. Let's go." He took the keys that Taryn handed him and ushered Stan to the door.

"I don—"

"Too bad." Seth snagged Laney's elbow and dragged her toward the stairs. She tugged against his hold, but his fingers were like silken vices. Not painful, but he sure wasn't letting go.

"We can't leave them up there," she panted as they ran down the first flight of stairs.

"They'll be fine."

"*I* won't be if we don't slow down," Stan called from the landing above.

Seth didn't slow down.

He dragged Laney down another flight and another, never even glancing up to see if Stan was following.

Stone cold. That's the expression that Seth wore. He didn't seem at all concerned about Stan falling farther and farther behind. He didn't seem concerned about Logan or Taryn either. Laney wasn't all that sure that he was concerned about his own safety because he seemed bent on breaking his neck and hers.

"What's going on?" she asked as Seth dragged her down the last flight and to the service door at the back.

"Just a feeling."

"Maybe you should have told everyone else about your feeling. Then maybe all five of us would be making our escape instead of just the two of us."

"Logan and Taryn will be fine. If we have to leave them behind, they'll make their way back to the safe house and meet up with us there."

"With what car?"

"Taryn is creative. She'll come up with something."

"What about Stan?"

"If he makes it down in time, I'll give him a ride. If he doesn't, he's on his own."

"I don't like this plan."

"I don't remember asking if you did." He shoved the door open and peered into the parking lot. Laney edged in close, catching a glimpse of watery sunlight and a few cars.

"What do you see?"

"Nothing that I'm worried about."

"But?"

"I still have a feeling. Stay here. I'll get the truck and pull it up to the door. You see anything concerning, take off. Otherwise, be ready to get out of here."

Take off where?

That's what she wanted to ask, but Seth disappeared, and she was left standing in the doorway, her heart hammering, her pulse racing. Footsteps pounded on the stairs above her. Stan or someone else?

She wasn't sure, and she didn't know if she should run out into the parking lot or run farther into the building. Maybe she should go out a front door and into another parking lot or hide in an office somewhere until the danger passed.

Whatever the danger was.

Seth hadn't been very specific about his feeling.

And it was taking him an awfully long time to get in the truck and drive around to pick her up.

She peered out the door but was afraid to open it too widely. For all she knew, a police officer was standing right on the other side of it.

That was the problem. She wasn't meant for this kind of drama. As a matter of fact, she'd have been content to spend her entire life sitting in front of swatches of fabric and piles of paint samples or walking through quiet antique stores choosing furnishings to refurbish for her clients.

The footsteps grew louder, and she backed away from the

door, glancing up the stairwell. Her heart jumped as she met Stan's eyes. Two flights up and staring straight down at her, his cheeks were flushed and the tufts of his hair stood up on his glossy head. He looked frantic, exhausted and oddly exhilarated, his eyes gleaming with excitement and, maybe, amusement.

"You go on without me, kid. I'll be fine," he called as the door flew open and Seth barreled in.

"I told you to be ready!" He grabbed her hand and started pulling her to the door.

"We can't leave Stan. He's almost here."

"I just saw a police car pull into the parking lot. You want to be in here when the police arrive?"

"No, but I don't want Stan to be here either. Or Taryn. Or Logan." *Please, God, don't let Logan get caught.* Of all of them, he had the most to lose and the most evidence stacked up against him.

"You think *I* do? We can all go down, or some of us can. The ones left standing will be the ones who eventually pick their fallen comrades up." He opened the door and shoved her into the truck.

"What about no man getting left behind? What about that?" She shifted, staring at the door to the building, willing it to open and Stan to walk out. Willing Logan and Taryn to be right behind him.

"That doesn't hold true unless you're in the military." He slammed her door, went back to the building and disappeared inside.

Seconds later, he was back out, Stan slung over his shoulder in a fireman carry.

"Put me down!" Stan sputtered as he was thrust into the truck.

"Gladly!" Then the engine roared, the truck took off and the door to the building flew open.

Not Logan.

Not Taryn.

A uniformed police officer, his hand on his gun holster.

"Step on the gas, rookie!" Stan shouted, and for once Seth didn't argue.

The truck peeled around the side of the building and swerved toward a police car parked near the main entrance.

"What are you doing?" Laney's heart beat so hard, she thought it would fly out of her chest.

"Giving them something to think about." He accelerated, the truck bouncing over a sidewalk and onto the street.

"Good plan. Now, how about you stop playing games and get us out of here?" Stan barked.

Seconds later, they were speeding down the highway, weaving in and out of traffic. Sirens screamed in the distance.

Seth didn't seem worried. He cut through a neighborhood and took a few side streets. If he cared that he'd left a co-worker behind, he didn't show it. If he was worried that they could be surrounded by police cars at any moment, Laney couldn't tell.

She cared, though, and she was worried. She wanted to jump out of the truck and go back to the building to find Logan and Taryn and make sure they were okay.

Please, let them be okay.

"He'll be fine, kid," Stan said, smoothing down his hair and glancing out the back window.

"It's not just Logan that I'm worried about. Taryn is back there, too."

"You have a soft spot for him, though, right?"

"No."

"Ha!"

"What's that supposed to mean?" she asked because she knew he expected her to. She didn't really have the heart for the conversation, though.

"It means that you two have a deep connection. I'd venture to say that you're even in love."

"Not even close."

"I know love when I see it, kid. I lived with the love of my life for forty years. She and I had a way of knowing when another couple had the kind of love that we shared. Even without her, I know forever love when I see it. You and Logan have it."

"We were friends as kids, Stan. That's all."

Seth snorted but didn't comment.

Good. The last thing Laney felt like doing was arguing with *both* men about something so ridiculous.

She and Logan in love?

She didn't even know what the word meant.

At least not when it referred to what she'd read about in books when she was a teenager—the kind of love that knocked the air from a woman's lungs and made her heart overflow with longing. That kind of love was the kind that could get a woman in trouble. The kind that could make her forget all the reasons why she needed to hold on to a little piece of her heart.

Not something that Laney had ever wanted.

All she'd wanted was the easy affection that she'd had for William. The undemanding acceptance that they'd had for each other. They'd been friends first, and they'd built a strong foundation from that. She'd believed with all her heart that it could sustain their marriage for a lifetime.

Maybe it would have.

Of course, it would have.

She'd chosen well, and if William hadn't gotten sick, she'd be living in their brownstone, content and happy to be his wife.

Wouldn't she?

"Did it work?" Stan whispered close to her ear.

"What?"

"My attempt to distract you?"

"If you were hoping that irritating me would distract me, then yes."

"Good." He grinned and settled back into his seat.

Two hours later she was still irritated and Stan was asleep, snoring softly, his lined face pale. Unanimated, he looked older, and she almost reached out to touch his wrist to check his pulse to make sure it was still beating strong and hard.

Her stomach ached with hunger and her head pounded with fatigue. Worry seemed to be gnawing a hole in her gut, and Seth just kept driving, his expression unreadable.

"Are we going to the safe house or crossing the country?" She broke the silence because she couldn't take one more second of it.

"Safe house. We're almost there. I just wanted to make sure we weren't followed."

"I think that you could have known that an hour and a half ago."

"Don't be so impatient, Laney. It could get you killed."

His words shivered through her as he pulled up in front of the little rancher. The garage door opened, and he pulled in. "Wake up, Pops, or we'll leave you out here sleeping."

Stan stirred, his dove-gray eyes opening. "Who says I was asleep, rookie? It might have been a ruse to see what the two of you had to say about me when you thought I wasn't listening."

"You were snoring," Seth responded dryly.

The two men seemed content to snap at one another. Laney only wanted one thing—for Logan and Taryn to show up.

"Do you think they made it out of the building?" She followed Seth into the house, and he nodded.

"I would have gotten a call from Darius if they'd been taken into custody."

"Maybe he hasn't had a chance to call."

"You worry a lot, Laney. You need to stop." He pulled the curtains across the front window. "I'm going to see what there is to eat. Don't know about the two of you, but I'm starving."

"How can you eat when—" The front doorknob rattled, and Laney froze, her blood cold and her muscles taut.

"Go into your bedroom and lock the door."

"What—"

"Go!" Seth shouted, his word reverberating through the house, through *her,* filling her with terror and spurring her into action.

She raced down the hall, slammed the door and locked it.

EIGHTEEN

She needed a weapon.

Just in case.

Seth might be tough and aggressive, but he was still just a man. A gun could take him down easily if the shooter had the opportunity. Once whoever was outside managed to get past him, Laney would be on her own because she didn't think Stan had it in him to protect either of them.

He'd try, though.

She knew he would.

Thinking about it made her chest tight.

She'd have to protect them both.

She'd find a weapon, climb out the window, reenter through the front door and come at the intruder from behind.

She spun around, frantic to find something she could use against an attacker. Aside from the pillows and a few books, there wasn't much in the room. She opened one of the dresser drawers and clawed through Taryn's clothes, feeling only slightly guilty. Nothing there. Nothing under the beds or under the mattresses. Didn't bodyguards keep extra weapons around?

Something creaked outside the door, the old wood floor giving way beneath heavy feet. Seth? Stan?

She didn't dare call out. She barely dared to breathe as she moved to the door and pressed her ear to the cool wood.

Nothing.

Not even a whispered word.

Another creak, and she froze, her blood running cold. If things were fine, Seth would be knocking already, giving her the all clear or grumbling for her to come out. She yanked the pillow from the bed, her palms sweaty with fear. She didn't know what she planned to do with it, but having it clutched close to her stomach felt better than having nothing.

The doorknob turned, and she backed toward the window, imagining a million scenarios, none of them ending well.

Were Stan and Seth both dead, their murderer on the other side of the door?

Could she climb out the window and leave without being noticed?

Could she abandon them if they were still alive and in danger?

She couldn't.

No way.

Ever.

She'd have to go around front.

She unlocked the window and eased it open a crack.

"Laney?" Logan called.

"Logan!" Her legs went weak with relief, but she managed to cross the room and yank the door open.

He stood on the other side of it, all lean, hard muscle and searing blue eyes. She wanted to step into his arms, burrow her head against his chest and tell him how terrified she'd been. She wanted to smooth his thick hair and feel the rough bristles of his five o'clock shadow beneath her palm.

She wanted all those things so much it almost hurt, and she fisted her hands and stepped back.

"Where have you been? I've been worried sick."

"So Seth said." He followed her across the room, settling onto the bed and pulling her down beside him. Leg to leg, arm to arm, shoulder to shoulder just the way they'd been so many times when they were kids.

Only they weren't kids anymore, and fire seemed to ignite everywhere they touched.

"Seth said something? He's barely spoken a dozen words to me and Stan since we left you guys."

"I guess he was saving up." He looked into her eyes. Really looked. Her pulse picked up speed as her body hummed with need.

She wanted so badly to throw herself into his arms. She wanted it more than she'd ever wanted just about anything.

She wrapped her arms around her waist, keeping them occupied while she tried to look anywhere but his face. "We saw the police back at the office building. I was worried that you and Taryn ran into them."

"Seth's stunt gave us just enough time to slip out the back. We walked a couple of miles and phoned a friend. He brought us a new ride."

"What's next?"

"We have some information to go through, and then I'm going back to Green Bluff. Christopher Banks and I are due to have a little meeting. Tonight will be as good a time as any for it."

"You can't go back there. It's way too dangerous."

"I have to, Laney."

"So that you can find the evidence that will prove your innocence to a bunch of people who don't matter?"

"They *do* matter. Green Bluff is my family. The only family I've had since Amanda passed away. It's my home. It's the place I've dreamed about every night since I was thrown into jail."

"It's also the place where everyone knows you. It's the

place where you've been judged and found guilty of something you didn't do."

"I'm going back."

"Why not just walk into the sheriff's department and turn yourself in, then?" She jumped up, pacing across the room, her irritation and worry making her desperate for movement and action.

"I may. After I talk to Banks."

"What are you talking about?" She made the mistake of looking straight into his eyes and felt her protest falling away, the world falling away.

This was the Logan of her childhood, but so much more than that, and she couldn't resist him. She could not seem to make herself look away.

"My friend spoke to the police this morning. The officer who survived the ambush refused to implicate me. Based on his testimony, the case against me may be reopened."

"The police could be lying to throw you off your guard."

"Do you really think that would work?" he answered, his tone as gentle as the fingers he trailed across her bruised cheek. "You need to put some more ice on this. Bring the swelling down a little."

"You're changing the subject."

"Maybe. I am, but I'm going back to Green Bluff, and I'm not taking you with me. Arguing about it won't change a thing."

"*Not taking me with you?* Did you really think you could slip that little piece of information in there without me noticing?"

"I had to give it a shot." He smiled, flashing his dimple.

"It's not funny."

"You're right. It's not, but the plans are made, and they're not going to change. You may as well just accept that."

"Accept that you and your buddies have made a decision

about my life without even consulting me? I don't think so, Logan. I got pulled into the trouble we're in, but that doesn't make me any less of a part of it than the rest of you. I should have an equal say in how we handle things."

She had a point, and Logan knew it.

He just didn't like it.

"Laney, you're here. You're safe. I want it to stay that way."

"What about what *I* want? Maybe Green Bluff is exactly where I want to be. When you're gone, maybe I'll head right back there. There won't be anyone to stop me. Taryn and Seth were contracted to protect you. They're going to be wherever you are. If you leave Stan with me, he'll be happy to find me a ride to Green Bluff. I can go back to the house my father left me. Get back to my life."

"And get yourself killed to prove a point?"

"This isn't about proving a point. This is about…" Her voice broke, and she looked away.

"What?" He cupped her shoulders, his gut clenching the way it did every time they touched.

A problem.

A big one, and he didn't know if he cared enough to solve it. He'd spent years mourning Amanda's death. Years telling himself that he'd never fail someone the way he'd failed her. Three years, and he'd never wavered from the course he'd set. Then he'd stumbled back into Laney's life, and all he could think about was how much he'd missed being part of it.

"It's about you, Logan. It's about how I'd feel if anything happened to you. It's about wanting to help you because we're friends." She looked away again, and he knew what she hadn't said, felt the response deep in his soul.

"Just friends?" He smoothed his hand down her arms and up again, watching as her eyes dilated and her lips parted slightly. He remembered how it felt to kiss those lips. He couldn't forget the feelings that had surged through him at the contact. It had been such a stupid mistake, kissing her to avoid detection, but he couldn't find it in himself to regret it.

"We were always more than that, weren't we? We were like family. Two parts of the same whole." She turned away, crossing the room and then spinning back to face him. "That scares me, Logan. If we're going to get right down to the heart of the matter, that's it. Everything about you is too much, and when I'm near you, I feel filled up with it. It's like I can't separate my emotions from you."

"Why would you want to?"

"Because I've been hurt a million times before. You, more than anyone else, know that. I don't want to be hurt again."

"Who says you will be?"

"Me. Life. Maybe even God."

"That's a pessimist's view."

"Is it pessimistic when you're speaking from past experience?"

"The past doesn't dictate the present or the future," he responded—and felt like a hypocrite.

"Right now it does. You can't go back to Green Bluff. Not if you want to keep your freedom."

"Keep it for what, Laney? My life is back there. Everything I've accomplished since your parents dragged me from the group home was accomplished there. Without it—"

"You're still you. You can make another life somewhere else."

"And every minute that I live of it will be a lie. That's not the way I want things to go down."

"I don't either, but I'd rather know you were alive somewhere living a lie than know you were dead. If you go to jail, that's what's going to happen, Logan. We both know it."

"I'm not going to keep running. Not forever. Not even for much longer. The police seem convinced that the ambush was a veiled attempt at kidnapping and murder. They're looking for suspects, and if they find them, I may be exonerated."

"They already have one suspect in custody." She brushed lint off her faded jeans, her hand shaking a little. He lifted it, studying her long, slender fingers and touching the deep scar on her knuckles.

Mildred had described it as an accident to the doctor. She and Laney had been cutting oranges together, and Mildred's knife had slipped. Laney had confirmed the story, but Logan had always wondered if it were the truth. At twelve, she'd been young enough to fear her mother and naive enough to believe that things would get better if she just tried harder and prayed enough.

"I have to do this, Laney. I know it scares you, but it's the way it has to be. I'm going to meet with Banks, and then I'm going to the sheriff's office."

"I want to go with you."

"We'll talk about it later, okay?"

"You mean when I wake up in the morning and you're gone, and the phone rings and it's you explaining that you left during the night?"

"I was kind of hoping that it would work out that way," he responded, and she cracked a smile, her eyes clear forest-green.

"At least you're honest."

"I try to be. Come on. We have a couple of file folders and a computer memory card to look through before we make the trip to Green Bluff."

"We?"

"Figure of speech."

"You know that I'm going. With or without you, right?"

He thought he did, thought that he'd have to tie her down to keep her from trying to help him.

"I wish you'd listen to reason, but I have a feeling you

won't." He sighed, and she touched his cheek and smiled into his eyes. She took his breath away with that simple gesture.

Her smile faltered, her hand falling from his cheek to his chest. He wasn't sure if she were trying to push him away or pull him closer.

"Logan…"

"You're beautiful, Laney. You know that?" He fingered a loose curl, let the silken strand slide between his fingers.

She was his old friend, and he thought that she might become so much more than that. If he let her.

The past can't dictate the present or the future. That's what he'd told her, but he seemed to be grasping the past with both hands, holding on tight, using it as an excuse to stay distanced from the harder things in life. The pain, the sorrow, the loneliness of loss. If he went to jail tomorrow and stayed there for the rest of his life, would he be happy that he'd done that, or would he think that he'd missed out on everything that could have been if he'd only taken a chance?

He bent toward Laney, wanting one more taste of her lips before he went back to Green Bluff. One more kiss, just in case this moment was the last memory of her that he'd ever have. A quick touch. That's all he meant it to be, but she sighed, her arms sliding around his waist, her fingers curved into his belt loops, and he couldn't make himself step away.

NINETEEN

She could stay in his arms forever.

The thought drifted through Laney's mind, wrapping around her heart in a fog of hunger that stole everything else away. Logic. Reason.

She pressed closer, wanting to inhale him the way she'd inhale the sweet scent of fresh-baked cookies or the warmth of the sunshine on the first day of spring.

"Logan! You coming to look at this stuff or not? Because I'm hungry and... Oops! Sorry." Taryn laughed, the sound splashing over the fire that seemed to burn in Laney's chest every time Logan was near.

She broke away and would have stepped from his arms, but he tightened his hold, his eyes blazing. "This isn't over."

She wasn't sure if it was a threat or a promise.

Either way, she was in trouble.

Because it didn't scare her.

She touched her lips, realized what she was doing and let her hand drop away.

"I think I'm hungry, too," she said because she could think of nothing else to say. *Had* nothing else to say.

One kiss she could explain away.

Two was more difficult.

She didn't even think she wanted to.

Logan nodded, his hands falling from her waist, his gaze following her as she ran past Taryn. She couldn't even look at the other woman. She could barely look at Stan as she walked into the kitchen.

"Where's Seth?" Laney asked, opening the fridge and hoping the cold air would cool her heated cheeks.

"I'm in here, staring at a bunch of papers that don't mean a whole lot and wondering why I'm looking at them alone," Seth growled from the small dining room that jutted off the back of the kitchen. It was probably an addition. The pale yellow walls and gleaming hardwood floor were the most updated thing in the house.

It was so much easier to think about that than about Logan. About his kiss.

Their kiss.

"You feeling okay, kid? You're awfully flushed. Maybe you've got a fever?" Stan pressed a cool palm to her heated cheeks, his gnarled hand calloused and rough from years of hard work.

"I'm fine. Just hungry."

"Good because I'm making some of my famous clam chowder. Minus the clams." He tossed chopped onion into a stew pot and stirred it with a wooden spoon.

"It can't be clam chowder without clams, Pops," Seth called out.

"Fish chowder, then, and if you keep interrupting while I'm working, you're not going to eat any of it."

"Work? Cooking fish stew isn't work. Work is poring over dozens of pages of documents while everyone else goofs off."

"I'll help." Laney grabbed a yogurt from the fridge and searched through the drawers until she found a spoon. She could hear Taryn and Logan moving toward the kitchen, and she didn't want to be anywhere in the vicinity when they arrived.

Fugitive

Not that she could avoid them in the little house, but she could at least be in a different room until she got her emotions under control. If she ever did. Which, when it came to Logan, seemed to be very difficult.

She carried the yogurt into the dining room and sat next to Seth. He'd spread dozens of pages across the dusty wood table. She reached for one.

"Not those. Look through these." He handed her a stack of pages. "Anything that has Danver's name on it goes in the pile on the right. Anything that mentions Banks goes in the middle. The left-hand pile is for anything that doesn't mention either of them."

"What about this pile?" She touched the one near the end of the table.

"That's iffy. I thought it was interesting how many Cascade Mountain Men members Brinkman has as clients."

"How many?"

"Taryn managed to access his computer system and download his files on to this." He held up a thumb drive. "I printed out the files, and a quarter of the cases Brinkman has worked in the past year are related to the group."

"How so?"

"He's a defense attorney. He defended the Mountain Men against charges that ranged from illegal firearms possession to disturbing the peace. Nothing big, though. Still, Danvers is a member of the group, and he showed up at your house. There's got to be a connection somewhere. We just have to find it."

"We will." Logan dropped into the chair beside Laney, stretching his long legs out under the table. He seemed completely at ease, the kiss they'd shared about as important to him as an ice cube at the North Pole.

"Did you make any arrests? Maybe give the group cause

to want to oust you from the police department?" Seth thrust a sheaf of paper into Logan's hand.

"None."

"I think we've already established that Banks is the connection. He and Mildred had a score to settle and he used his partner's clients to make it happen." Taryn sat across from Seth and opened a laptop.

"Too bad speculation isn't enough to convict a man," Seth muttered.

"We have more than speculation." Taryn frowned and dropped a page onto one of the piles.

"But not enough to bring before a jury." Logan rubbed the back of his neck, and Laney clenched her fist, remembering the way his skin felt...rough and warm and wonderfully familiar.

"Brinkman is a lawyer with a good reputation for getting the job done. I'm on his website now. Lots of wonderful recommendations from enthusiastic clients. I wonder how happy he'd be to know what Banks has been up to. Maybe we should call him and ask," Taryn responded, her head bent close to the computer screen.

"Let's let the police handle that. Assuming that he wasn't involved, I'm pretty sure that Brinkman will be happy to cooperate with an investigation. I'm going to use the desktop. I think I can replace the existing memory card with the one I took from Banks's system." Logan moved to a small computer desk shoved against the wall and dragged the hard drive from beneath it.

Everyone in the room seemed focused and busy. Except for Laney. She just sat with the papers Seth had given her still clutched in her hand.

She wanted to think it was because she wasn't a police officer or a security specialist or anything else that would prepare her to look for clues and evidence, but really, it was because of Logan.

She glanced at the paper at the top of her pile, trying to read the words. They were black letters against a white background. No meaning at all to them.

"Find anything interesting?" Logan asked, and she met his eyes. She realized a moment too late that she shouldn't have. Fire simmered in the depth of his gaze, and she felt it in the depth of her heart. Laney felt that little piece that she held on to so tightly slipping from her grasp.

"Laney?" He raised a dark eyebrow.

"I'm not sure what I'm looking for." She knew her cheeks were red, could feel the heat drifting up her face.

"Let me see." He held out a hand, and she gave him the pages, her fingers brushing his, all the longing she tried to keep hidden from the world and from herself pooling in her belly.

"I think I'll go help Stan." She walked from the room even though she wanted to run, and she didn't look back to see if Logan was watching her retreat despite being tempted to do just that.

Move on. Start fresh. That had been her plan from the very beginning of her journey back to Green Bluff. Logan was part of the past. He couldn't be part of the future.

Could he?

"What's got your knickers in a wad, kid?" Stan looked up from the stew pot, his face wrinkled with age and experience. Laney had never known her grandparents, but when she was a kid, she'd imagined having extended family. Aunts and uncles and grandparents who'd give her a place to stay that was far away from her parents' abuse. In her mind, her grandfather had been something like Stan. White-haired and easygoing. The kind of man who said what he meant and meant what he said.

"I don't think I'm much of an asset when it comes to looking for evidence. I thought maybe I could help you with the stew."

"It's all in the pot, and I was just heading into the dining room. You come on in with me. I'll help you figure things out."

"It's okay. I'll just stay in here and…" She looked around. "Wash the dishes." There was one—a coffee mug sitting in the sink.

"You avoiding something, doll?" Stan smoothed the white tufts of his hair. "Or, maybe, someone?"

"Just trying to stay out of the way."

"Hmm."

"What's that supposed to mean?"

"Just means that if you were my granddaughter, I'd tell you to stop being so afraid and follow your heart."

"I'm not—"

"I'd better go help those dunderheads. Otherwise, they might miss something important."

"We heard that, Pops," Seth called out, and Stan smiled.

"I meant you to." He walked into the dining room and left Laney standing at the sink, staring down at the lone cup. She washed it quickly, stirred the soup and listened to the mumbled conversation going on in the dining room.

If she were honest, she'd admit she wanted to go sit next to Logan and watch while he fiddled with the computer and found the information he was looking for. She'd admit that being with him felt better than being alone ever had.

And his kiss… It had shaken her. Made her long for something more than the life she'd been planning.

A dangerous thought. One that she might be sorry for when this was all over, and she went back to her life and Logan went back to his.

That *was* what was going to happen.

If everything worked out the way it should.

Logan free. Laney back in Seattle, back at her job, doing what she loved.

Alone.

She'd never thought about how heavy that word was, how hard it was to hold.

Someone walked into the kitchen behind her. She didn't turn. Didn't have to. She knew it was Logan. She felt him like rain on parched desert sand.

"Stan said that I need to stir the stew," he said, his voice rumbling out and wrapping around her.

"I already did."

"He also said that a pretty woman like you shouldn't be all alone when there were five people in the house."

"He could have sent Taryn in." She finally turned, resting her hip against the counter.

"He could have, but he seems to think that we're a couple."

"I noticed that."

"We could be."

"For this moment? While we're stuck in a safe house with nowhere to go and no one else to lean on?"

"You know that's not what I mean, Laney." He stepped closer, and her whole body wanted to move toward him.

"What else is there? You're a police officer in a town that I promised myself I'd never return to, and I have a life in Seattle."

"I'm not a police officer there anymore."

"But you want to return. You said so yourself."

"And you said that you were thinking about keeping the house, remember?"

"That doesn't mean that I'll live in it. Just that I'll hold on to it for the family."

"What family, Laney? How can there be one if you're not there?" His gaze drifted to her lips, and she shivered.

"I—"

He was right, and she knew it, but there was nothing she could say in response.

Family was all she'd ever wanted. All she'd cared about when she was young, but she couldn't be a family by herself. No one could. Her eyes burned with the thought, her throat tight with a thousand memories and dozens of dead dreams.

"I guess you don't have anything to say to that?" Logan stared into her eyes, and she thought that if she were a little braver, she'd tell him exactly what she wanted, needed, hoped for.

"The house is too big for one person."

"So, fill it with people."

"How? I don't want to raise children alone, and after William died, I decided that I wouldn't marry again."

"I thought the same thing after Amanda passed away. I'd failed her, and I didn't want to risk failing someone else I loved. I've realized something, though. Life without risk is lonely. Life without challenges is boring. When this is over, I don't want to live the safe and comfortable life I created for myself. I want something more."

With you.

He didn't say it, but Laney heard the words. They echoed in her heart, and she wanted to hold on to them, believe in them.

"You're braver than I am, Logan," she said. "You always have been."

"Not brave—just sure of what I want."

"I—"

"Good news." Stan walked into the room, and Laney backed away from Logan, her hip gouged by the counter, her heart tripping and jumping.

"What?" Logan's gaze never left her face, and Laney thought that if she were just brave enough, she might be able to have everything she'd ever wanted.

"Chris had Danvers's contact information in his email address book. I found two emails in his sent file. Nothing in the deleted files, but I guess he was smart enough to get rid of those."

"What did he say in the emails?" Logan's gaze shifted, and Laney eased out from between him and the counter.

"How about I tell you over some fish chowder? Grub's on! You want to eat, you'd better come now," Stan shouted in the direction of the dining room.

Seconds later, Seth and Taryn appeared, both looking triumphant.

Good news, and Laney was excited to hear it.

She just wasn't sure how excited she was going to be when this was over and she went back to Seattle.

She would go back.

She had to.

Her life was there.

Everything she'd worked for was there.

When she looked at Logan, though, watched as he took a computer printout from Stan, she couldn't help wondering if having the things she'd worked for was ever again going to be enough.

TWENTY

"Are you nuts? She's a civilian." Logan slapped his hand on the table with enough force to shake his nearly empty bowl of chowder. He didn't care. No way was he going along with the plan Seth had just outlined.

"If we're going to split hairs, so are you." Seth ladled more chowder into his bowl. He seemed completely unaffected by Logan's outburst.

He was going to be affected really soon if he didn't stop suggesting that Laney be the one to visit Chris Banks.

"Getting tossed in jail didn't undo all my years of training. I may not be wearing a badge, but I'm still a police officer."

"Then why are you letting your heart rule your head?" Seth eyed him over his fresh bowl of chowder.

"The only thing I'm being ruled by is logic. It makes no sense for Laney to be sacrificed to the cause."

"I'm not going to be sacrificed. I'm just going to ask Chris a few questions. Like Seth said, I'm the least threatening in the group, and Chris and I have already talked. He may be more open to me than to anyone else." Laney swirled a spoon around in her uneaten stew, the bruise on her cheek fresh and vivid.

"That doesn't mean he's not going to shoot you the second you show up at his house."

"I won't show up there. I'll ask him to meet me—"

"What you're going to do—"

"You're not about to get all macho on us, are you, Randal? Because that won't be a good look for you." Taryn washed her bowl and put it in the drainer, a glint of amusement in her eyes.

Logan wasn't amused.

"What's macho about wanting to protect an innocent bystander? Isn't that part of all of our jobs?" He kept his voice steady and his tone light. He'd learned the power of self-control a long time ago, and he refused to allow circumstances to take that from him.

"None of us are going to have jobs if we can't prove your innocence. You've got to remember, pal, that your future isn't the only one on the line here. We were all at Mildred's place, and it's not like we tried to disguise ourselves." Taryn dug through a cupboard and took out a package of chocolate chip cookies.

She had a point, and that irritated him.

He couldn't risk Laney's life, but he couldn't allow two innocent people to lose everything for him either. Three if he counted Stan. Although he had a feeling the older guy was anxious to lose at least part of what he'd left behind.

"What are your thoughts, Stan?" He asked because the older man had been a police officer for thirty years and had a wealth of experience to pull from.

Stan looked up from the printed emails he was still studying and grinned. "I thought you'd never ask, kid."

"You were going to give your thoughts to us anyway, Pops, whether we asked for them or not. So, how about you get to it?" Seth growled, but he grabbed Stan's bowl and ladled more stew into it.

"Don't mind if I do." Stan smiled again, but Logan didn't miss the hard edge in his eyes or the excitement in his voice.

He might have retired a few years ago, but he was still a police officer through and through. "I've been thinking about this while the four of you argued, and it's clear that we have a problem."

Seth sighed loudly and snagged a cookie from the package. "These emails link Chris and Danvers, but that doesn't prove any crime, does it?" He glanced at each one of them as if they were schoolkids, and he wanted to make sure they got the point.

Logan did, and he was pretty certain everyone else at the table did, too. The emails seemed like everyday correspondences between an attorney and client. Except that Banks and Danvers weren't attorney and client.

He snagged the sheets and read them again.

The first one confirmed a court date.

The second confirmed a meeting at a restaurant in Seattle.

"No crime, but I'd like to see what Danvers's bank account looked like before and after these two dates." If Logan hadn't been in such hot water, he'd have phoned Tanner and asked him to look into it.

"I already passed the information on to Darius, and he's contacted Officer Parsons." Taryn leaned back in her chair and stared up at the ceiling. "You were saying, Stan?"

"I was saying that the problem is lack of evidence. We can get it, though. Chris is too smart for his own good. He doesn't believe that anyone can match wits with him and win. Those emails are a perfect example of it." He waved toward the pages that Logan held. "If Laney puts on the right show, he'll want to be part of it."

"What do you mean?" Laney poured the remainder of her stew into the sink, her hair spilling down her back in a riot of curls that begged to be touched. Maybe Seth was right. Maybe Logan *was* allowing his heart to rule his head.

He frowned.

He didn't allow emotion to rule. Not when it came to his job. "What's your idea, Stan?"

"All Laney has to do is act like she wants to bring you down. A few compliments to stroke Chris's ego, and he'll be pulling her right into his plan."

"You really think he's going to be that easy?" Seth grabbed another cookie, but he looked interested. Logan was, too. Neither of them knew Banks as well as Stan did.

"Not easy, but I think she can convince him if she plays it right. Look at Mildred. She got that boy thinking you lied about everything, Logan. Made him believe that she was falsely accused, that you and Josiah formed an alliance the day you met and that you were in deep with his schemes. As a matter of fact, she was pretty vocal about all the wealth you'd amassed and hidden in an offshore account somewhere before you got the police involved."

"That's quite a story for someone to buy into." Logan swallowed down bitterness. Half of the community he loved had bought into a story that was just as fantastic. No sense in holding on to it, but it still burned the back of his throat and settled like hot lava in his stomach.

"Exactly. When I heard it, I told her she was nuts. Weren't you only fourteen when you arrived in Green Bluff?"

"Right."

"A kid, and she was talking about you like you were a hardened criminal."

"I did have a juvenile record."

"Beside the point." Stan waved his hand like he could wave the idea away. "All I had to do was a little research to find out that you'd been a good citizen for longer than you hadn't been. Chris could have done the same. He didn't. He wanted to believe Mildred. He did. End of story."

"Good to know, but we can't risk Laney's life on the chance that he'll want to believe *her,* too."

"No, but I think that there's more than a chance. See, Mildred has spent the past couple of years convincing Chris that Laney was brainwashed into thinking she was a horrible mother. In Mildred's stories, she tried her best to give Laney the life she deserved but was so abused herself, she couldn't manage. Poor, weak-minded Laney didn't stand a chance."

Laney snorted.

"Obviously complete hogwash, but in Chris's mind, you're easily influenced, maybe a little confused, but still an innocent bystander in everything. We can use that to our advantage," Stan continued gleefully.

"Maybe, but I'm no actress, and I don't think I could convince Chris of anything. The most I could do is ask a few questions and hope he trips up answering them." Laney frowned. She seemed disappointed. Logan wasn't. He didn't want her anywhere near Banks.

"You won't have to convince him of anything. That's the beauty of the thing. Chris already believes that Logan is scum, and he knows that you're family. All you have to do is show up at his place in the middle of the night. He's got a wife and kids. He's not going to knock you off in front of them. Cry a few tears. Tell him that Logan abandoned you after he used you to escape. Say that you're scared and you don't want to go to jail. The last part is true, and maybe you could even get a few tears going if you think about it enough."

"She's not going to Green Bluff," Logan cut in.

"Says who?" Laney's eyes flashed green fire, her lips pressed together in a warning that Logan had no intention of heeding.

"Me."

"It's been a long time since I didn't do something just because someone else said that I shouldn't."

"Let's not bicker, kids. There's a perfect solution to this problem." Taryn sounded amused. That seemed to be her normal state of being, though Logan was sure there was something dark in her eyes. Secrets and hidden sorrows. They were in Laney's, too, buried almost too deep to see.

"What's your definition of perfect?" Logan washed his bowl and spun to face the group. He seemed to be the lone opposition to the plan.

His heart ruling his head.

He couldn't shake the thought that he was doing exactly what Seth had accused him of. He also couldn't make himself care.

"We do exactly what Stan suggested."

"No way. I told you—"

"Hear me out, Logan." Taryn cut him off, her voice sharp and hard-edged. Not as soft and smiley as she seemed to want people to think.

"We'll get what we need to wire Laney up. We'll be close enough that we can be there in seconds if she needs us. She won't need us, though. She'll be at Banks's house, and she won't leave there with him. Will you, Laney?"

"No," Laney answered quickly, her voice shaking just a little.

"This isn't a good idea. If Banks realizes she's lying, he could kill her before we have a chance to move in," Logan said.

"With his family in the house? I don't think so. Besides, we'll be stationed outside the house. It won't take long to get to her. She can have a nice little chat with Banks, convince him that she wants you punished. Hopefully, that will be enough to get the arrogant jerk talking."

"And if it isn't, we've risked Laney's life for nothing."

"There's not a whole lot of risk if Chris's wife and kids are around. As long as Laney doesn't leave with him, she'll be fine. Besides, Chris won't want to get his hands dirty."

Stan sounded confident, and if Laney had been anyone else, Logan might have been fully on board.

But she wasn't anyone else, and he couldn't stomach the thought of sending her into the lion's den on the hope that the lion's mouth would be sealed shut. He wanted to *know* it was sealed. He would have been happy to seal it himself.

"I still think it's too risky."

"Aren't you the guy who told me that life without risks is—"

"I know what I told you," he bit out, cutting Laney off because she was right. He knew it. Without risk, they'd accomplish nothing. He just didn't want to risk *her*.

"I'll agree there's a slight risk," Seth said. "But it's not like she's going to be alone. We'll be right outside. If anything goes wrong, we'll run in to save the day."

"What if she's dead before we manage to do that?"

"I won't be." Laney hoped. As eager as she was to prove Logan's innocence, she really didn't want to die.

And she really wasn't a good actress.

As a matter of fact, she was a really bad one.

She'd auditioned for school plays every year because her mother had wanted her to. The most she'd ever gotten was a walk-on part, and that was just because the drama teacher felt sorry for her.

"It's a good plan. If we were using anyone else as bait, you'd be all for it, Randal," Stan said.

Laney wasn't sure she liked the word "bait." Especially not when it referred to her.

"You're right. I'm not going to deny it." Logan smoothed his hair and ran his hand down his jaw, his gaze fixed on her. She shivered, her mind going back to the moment when his lips had touched hers, when his hands had been warm and firm on her waist. The moment when she would have given anything to be able to stay right where she was forever.

She was scared, but she'd risk anything to give him his freedom.

"I'll be fine," she said because she knew he needed to hear it and because she needed to hear it, too.

"Well, that's settled, so I think I'll go get a few things together for our drive to Green Bluff. Never been there, but Mildred said it was nice." Stan stood, his age-spotted hands pushing against the table.

"What kind of things do you need, Pops? Maybe, I can help you get them." Seth stood and stretched. It seemed that the meeting had been adjourned, the decisions made.

Laney should be thrilled, but she was terrified.

"This'll do." Stan pulled a butcher knife out of a drawer. "I can sharpen this baby up real nice."

He hurried from the room.

"That old man is going to get himself killed," Seth muttered and followed.

"I'd better get a few things done, too. Darius needs to be updated on the plan. We'll leave here around nine. That figures a four-hour drive back to Green Bluff, an hour or so of prep, and we should have Laney knocking on Banks's door around two in the morning. That'll throw him off his stride a little, and that's exactly what we want." Taryn collected all the pages from the table, her movements quick and easy. She didn't look at all nervous about the plan.

Laney wished she had that kind of confidence. Not just in herself, but in God, in the people around her. In the idea that things would always work out for the best if she just had faith.

"You sure that you want to do this?" Logan asked as Taryn left the kitchen.

Was she?

All Laney knew was that she couldn't spend the rest of her life believing that she could have helped Logan and hadn't.

"Yes."

"Then make sure you're doing it for the right reasons, okay?" His hands skimmed up her arms and rested on her shoulders. She could feel every finger burning through her T-shirt. She could feel the weight of his palms, comforting and familiar.

She loved him.

The thought speared into her heart and took hold of the emptiness there.

She shoved it away because there were all kinds of love, and she only wanted to give Logan the kind she'd given him when they were kids.

"I am."

"So, you're not doing it for me? You don't have some misguided notion about repaying me for what I did when you were a kid?"

"No." Actually, she *did* have the notion, but it wasn't misguided.

"Then what is your motivation, Laney? What are you going to get out of this?"

"Justice?" It sounded like a good answer, but she wasn't sure she said it forcefully enough to be convincing.

"For me? Because if that's the case—"

"This isn't all about you anymore. Seth, Taryn and Stan need this to work, too. We all have our freedom riding on what happens tonight." She sidestepped the question, and she knew that he noticed. His eyes narrowed and his lips pressed together in a firm line.

He looked dangerous and angry and more handsome than any man had a right to look.

Love.

She'd wanted it so desperately for so many years. She'd wanted it when she'd met William, but she'd wanted it on her terms. She had wanted it enough to risk something but not everything.

With Logan, she'd have to risk it all.

She stepped back, swallowing down words that she couldn't allow herself to say. "It's going to be a long night. I think I'd better lie down for a while."

She didn't wait for his response, just ran from the room like the coward she was beginning to realize that she was.

TWENTY-ONE

Two in the morning came way too soon.

At least in Laney's mind it did. Everyone else seemed excited, the air in the truck charged with energy. *Laney* was terrified.

"Ready?" Logan squeezed her hand. She wanted to hold on tight. Refuse to get out when the truck pulled up at the end of Chris's street.

"I think so."

"You'd better know so, kid. This is no time to get nervous." Stan patted her knee as they wound through Green Bluff's ritziest neighborhood. The yards were large, two or three acres, and well lit by streetlights. People with money lived there. People who kept their yards perfect and their homes pristine. People who might notice Laney walking down the middle of the street and call the police.

She swallowed the acid at the back of her throat.

"She'd be a fool if she wasn't nervous, Stan," Taryn said easily as she pulled to the side of the road. "This is it, Laney. You, Logan and Seth get out here. Stan and I will park on the street behind this one. If you have any trouble, scream, and we'll let the boys know. They'll be there to help you in two shakes of a stick."

Great. Except that Laney was pretty sure shaking a stick

would take longer than firing a bullet. If Chris had a gun and decided to use it, she'd be dead before either of the men could get to her.

She kept the thought to herself and got out of the truck. Cold air bathed her face and seeped through her coat. The small microphone that Taryn had taped under her shirt felt cool and hard against her skin. It was a small comfort, but at least she had it.

Logan and Seth hopped out of the truck behind her.

"Let's go." Logan took her arm, leading her to a large pine tree that stood at the edge of an oversize yard. The house it belonged to was dark as pitch and shielded from the street by large shrubs. He stopped there, his eyes gleaming in the darkness.

"Stick to the plan, Laney. Go straight to Banks's house. Don't stop for anything on the way there. Seth and I will be close, but we need to stay out of sight. By the time you get to his house, we'll be in the backyard," Logan whispered, and the chill of his words made her heart thump painfully. Not only was she going to do this, but also she was basically doing it alone. Sure, she had backup close by, but all the acting? That was hers, and she really wasn't sure she was going to be successful.

"Okay." She wiped her sweaty palms on her jeans.

"Are you sure? Because there's still time to back out if you don't think you can do this."

She wasn't. Not by a long shot. But she had to do it. For herself and the team. Maybe even for redemption. She'd fled Green Bluff thirteen years ago and left Logan to clean up the mess her parents had made. It was her turn to do the cleaning, and she wasn't going to run away from that. No matter how much she wanted to.

"I can do it."

"All right. Let's get moving." He dropped a quick kiss to her lips and stepped away from the tree.

That was her cue to move, and her feet did what they were supposed to even as her mind screamed for her to stop and think things through a little more.

She'd memorized Chris's address and had studied satellite photos of the property, but everything looked different in the darkness, the trees dark shapes against a deep gray sky, the houses hulking buildings without character or color.

She walked down the middle of the street just the way the team had planned, knowing that a dog could bark or a person might peer out a window and see her. Unlike Logan and Seth, she had no reason to stay hidden.

Four houses up to the left. Laney counted each one, her heart beating louder with every step. Could Taryn and Stan hear it pounding?

She stopped in front of a two-story Greek revival and read the street address on the mailbox even though she knew she was in the right place. Avoidance. Procrastination. She was pretty good at both those things, but she couldn't put this off. She walked up the driveway, her feet padding on the pavement, the early-morning silence eerie.

Were Seth and Logan in place?

Were Taryn and Stan?

She hesitated at the front door, her hands still sweaty and her lips still tingling from the kiss Logan had pressed to them. If he were there, he'd already have rung the doorbell, would probably be inside the house questioning Chris.

Please, God, let this work.

Please.

She rang the doorbell, jumping a little as it pealed through the interior of the house. Not a subtle doorbell, that was for sure. She rang it again for good measure.

Light spilled out from a second-story window. More light

splashed through the windows on either side of the door. Laney tensed, waiting for the door to fly open and trying to remember what she was supposed to say.

She'd gone over it dozens of times with Taryn and dozens more with Logan. Even Seth and Stan had drilled her. She knew the script. She hoped.

"Who's there?" Someone called through the closed door.

Chris? She really hoped so. It would be a shame to have wasted all her nerves on the wrong house.

"Laney Jefferson." She managed to get her name out and stepped back so that the speaker could see her through the peephole.

The door opened so suddenly, she nearly screamed.

"Laney? What are you doing here?" Chris's hair stood on end, his flannel pajama top only half buttoned, a thick robe hanging limply from his tall frame.

She'd definitely woken him. That had been part of the plan. The next part was to get him talking.

"I'm in trouble." The first line in the script came as easy as could be.

"I'll say you are. The Green Bluff police have been all over town looking for you. The Seattle police and the state police are involved, too." He stepped back, gesturing for her to enter.

She really didn't want to. There was something about the way he kept looking up and down the road that made the hair on her nape stand on end.

"Maybe we should talk out here. I wouldn't want to wake your wife and kids."

Stick to the script! She could almost hear Logan whisper, but her gut was saying stay outside, and that's exactly what she planned to do.

"They're not home. I sent them to visit my wife's parents when things went nuts this morning."

"Things?"

Had Taryn and Stan heard that she and Chris were alone? Was the mike working? She clenched her fists to keep from touching it.

"I got home from my business trip this morning and found the police sitting in my living room."

"I'm sorry, Chris. I never meant to cause you any trouble."

"I know you didn't, and I'm not blaming you. But my wife and kids were upset, and I thought it would be better for them to get out of town for a while. Come on. Let's go inside where it's warmer." He grabbed her arm, his grip just a little too tight, and pulled her inside.

The door closed with a quiet click, and he slid the lock home. "I guess you need my help?"

"I…" She fumbled for the next part of the script, then found it. "Logan contacted me, and I couldn't make myself turn him away. I drove him to Seattle to visit my mother because he said she was the key to his troubles. He left me in the middle of the city. I've been trying to get back here since yesterday afternoon."

"You didn't call the police for help? That would have been the logical thing to do."

"I didn't want to be thrown in jail."

"It may happen anyway. You know that, right? What you did was a crime, and you can't expect the authorities to ignore that."

"I know, and I know that I shouldn't have helped Logan, but he's an old friend, and he told me that he was innocent." Her voice broke, and she didn't even have to try to make it happen. She was so terrified that her body vibrated with it, but Chris didn't seem to notice.

"Come into my office and have a seat. Let's discuss things rationally and see what we come up with."

She went because, short of screaming bloody murder and

bringing Logan and Seth in before she'd learned anything helpful, she didn't have a choice.

Chris led her through a living room, dining room and kitchen. A family room jutted off from there, a few toys lying on the floor. The whole house was as opulent as his office in Seattle had been. Gleaming wood floors and antique furniture. Oil paintings on the walls and handwoven throw rugs on the floor.

"My office is through here." He opened doublewide doors that led into a large room.

"This is at the back of the house, right?" she asked, because if Logan and Seth needed to get to her quickly, she wanted them to know where to look.

"Yes. Why?"

"I was just thinking it must be a nice quiet place to work because it's away from the street. Most of the houses I decorate have the offices in the front." She was babbling, and that was going to get her into trouble if she wasn't careful.

"It's a quiet neighborhood, so there isn't a lot of noise from the street. I do have a nice view of the yard, though, and access to the back deck. I like to work out there sometimes. Go ahead and sit down. Do you want anything? Tea? Coffee?"

"No. Thanks." She settled onto the edge of a high-backed leather chair, and he took a seat across from her.

"You've really gotten yourself into a mess, Laney. You know that, don't you?"

"That's why I'm here. I didn't know who else to turn to."

"I'm not a criminal lawyer, but I'll do what I can to help you. Your father was my client, after all."

"I appreciate it."

"Now that we've got that out of the way, why don't you tell me what happened?"

"Logan was staying at my parents' place. I didn't know it until I arrived. I didn't kick him out. I couldn't." The truth was so easy, and she could tell that Chris was eating it up. He leaned toward her, his eyes hard hazel pebbles.

"He was there when I visited?"

"Yes."

"And when the sheriff stopped by?"

"Yes."

"This isn't going to look good for you, Laney."

"I know. The problem is, I always looked up to Logan when I was a kid. I thought he was some kind of hero when he helped me leave town. When he showed up in my life again, I wanted to help him." Truth, truth and more truth.

"I can understand that."

"Logan planned to leave because he didn't want me to get into trouble with the police, but a guy broke into my house and attacked me. The next thing I knew, I was driving across the state with a bunch of people I didn't know, and Logan was telling me that it was the only way to stay safe. Now, I think that he just wanted to make sure that I didn't tell the police anything before he had a chance to escape." Lie! Her face felt flushed with it, but Chris just leaned in closer.

"He left you in Seattle, right?"

"I didn't even have a dollar on me."

"Sounds like the kind of guy Logan is."

"What do you mean?" Was it really going to be this easy? Was he really going to fall right into the plan and start confessing his hatred of Logan and his desire for revenge?

"Logan Randal is liar and a thief, Laney. If the crimes he was convicted of aren't enough to convince you of that, take a look at his juvenile record. They clearly show a kid who was heading for trouble. He hit Green Bluff, and he found it."

"He was a straight-A student and worked two jobs. He volunteered as a Special Olympics coach and helped kids train in track and field. How is that finding trouble?" She jumped to Logan's defense without thought, and Chris scowled.

"Every word he said about your mother was a lie. He set her up and hoped she'd go to prison and rot. If you ask me, when he went to jail, he was finally getting his just deserts."

"You're probably right."

"There is no probably about it. I know that you and your mother had your differences, but she's a good woman who has had a tough life. She suffered a lot of loss, and losing her freedom was just one more cross she had to bear." His words sounded so much like something Mildred would say that Laney stood, pacing to French doors that looked out over the dark yard. She couldn't look in Chris's eyes. She didn't even want to look into his face, afraid that if she did, she'd let the truth spill out—tell him just how wrong he was, just how used he'd been.

A shadow swayed near a tall pine tree, the movement making Laney's heart jump.

Logan, her heart whispered. She wanted to reach through the cold glass and grab hold of his strong and comforting hand.

It was a silly notion, but she could almost feel the warmth of his calloused palm. She had to do this. She had to convince Christopher that she wanted Logan punished as much as he did. It was the only way to save the man who'd once saved her.

"You're right," she said. "When Logan went after my family, I was young and naive. I wanted to believe in knights in shining armor. I'm way past that stage. I know there are no real heroes." That was not part of the script, but she knew Chris bought it. She could feel him looming over her, coming in close. His arm dropped around her shoulder, and it was all she could do not to jerk away.

"I'm glad you've finally seen the light, Laney. It's too bad it's too late." His words were ice water in her veins, and she jerked back and looked into his empty eyes.

"Too late? I thought you said you were going to try to help me."

"I am. But probably not in the way you'd hoped." His eyes were feverishly bright, and she stepped back, her body rigid with fear.

"What are you talking about?"

"I'm going to make sure you never have to worry about Logan again."

He lunged, pulling something from his robe pocket and shoving it against her neck.

She felt a moment of stark terror and then she felt nothing at all.

TWENTY-TWO

"We've lost contact." Taryn's terse words drifted through Logan's radio.

He didn't wait to hear more. He just ran toward the house. Seth met him halfway across the yard, gun already in hand, his face set and hard.

"Front or back?" he barked.

"Go in the French doors. I'll go around the front." Logan swerved around the side of the house, his blood running cold as an engine roared to life. Headlights splashed on Banks's driveway, and a dark sedan pulled out of the garage. Slow and easy, like the driver had all the time in the world.

Logan pulled his gun and aimed for the sedan's tires. One shot, and the car swerved but didn't stop.

The driver stepped on the gas, pushing the sedan to its limit.

"He's in a dark blue sedan heading east on Baker. I shot out one of his tires, but he's not slowing down," Logan shouted into his radio, running out onto the road and firing another shot. The neighbor's lights went on and a dog barked, but he didn't care.

There was no response from Taryn, and Logan wanted to shout into the radio again.

Footsteps pounded on the road behind him, and he turned and met Seth's eyes. "He's got her."

"Good thing our ride is here then." Seth gestured to the truck that was squealing around the corner. Taryn braked a few feet away, and Logan and Seth jumped in.

"I've already called the sheriff's department and reported the kidnapping. Just so you know, we're all going down if Banks gets away. I used your name to get people moving, and I think the sheriff's department is more concerned with catching you than they are with finding Laney."

"I don't care what they're concerned about as long as they get here quickly."

"Exactly what I was thinking." Taryn stepped on the gas, and the truck raced along the dark road, flying up a hill and around a curve in the road. Up ahead, brake lights glowed and disappeared.

"He turned off," Stan muttered. "Anyone know where that road leads?"

"Spokane Mountain Park," Logan responded.

"Plenty of places to hide a body, I bet," Seth growled.

"She's not a body yet. The mike is still picking up signals, and I'm pretty sure I heard Laney mumble something," Taryn said.

Thank you, God.

All they had to do was get to her, make sure that she stayed alive.

The truck shimmied to the left, nearly bouncing off the road and into a ravine as Taryn turned onto the park road.

"Watch what you're doing, kid. We lose our ride, and we lose Laney," Stan snapped, his head bent close to the window, one hand clutching the door handle, the other pressing a cell phone close to his ear. "Anyone have an address? The 911 operator wants to know."

Logan rattled it off, his body humming with the need for action, his eyes glued to the distant taillights. There. Then gone.

"Pull over," he ordered.

"What?" Taryn eased off the gas, but she didn't stop.

"He's either decided to stop or he's broken an axle and had to. If he sees us coming, there's no telling what he'll do. So, *pull over*."

Taryn braked hard, turned off the engine and cut the lights. In the sudden silence, Logan could hear the faint sound of pursuit. Sirens but not close enough to save Laney.

He jumped out of the truck, cold wind biting through his jacket as he started up the steep hill. Snowflakes fell from the steel-gray sky, landing on his face and sliding down into his collar. For a moment, he was back on the mountain, running from the wrecked police cruiser, chains on his wrists. He hadn't known where he was running to. Now he realized that he'd been running back home, to the place where he'd built his dreams then lost them. Now, maybe, he could find them again.

Had found them again. In Laney's eyes. In her arms. In the sweet feel of her body pressed to his.

Seth grabbed his arm and dragged him to the side of the road. "You can't go running in there half-cocked. You'll get yourself *and* Laney killed."

"If we don't hurry, she *will* be killed." He shrugged away, keeping to the shadowy edges of the road, letting the darkness hide him as he ran through the thickening snow.

Please, God. Don't let me fail again. Please.

The prayer burst from the depth of his soul, echoing in the stillness.

Up ahead, the dark sedan sat abandoned in the middle of the road. Lights off, driver's door open. Banks had to be somewhere, but Logan was more worried about finding Laney.

"Check the trunk. I'll see if I can figure out which direction Banks headed. We'd both better hurry because from the sound of those sirens, I'd say we'll be in handcuffs in about ten minutes." Seth went to the front of the car and flashed a light on the ground while Logan popped the trunk. He looked inside, hope and dread filling him.

Nothing but a dark splotch on the pristine interior.

He frowned, leaning close. Blood. He knew what it looked like, the scent. He also knew it had to be from Laney, and his stomach heaved, every nightmare he'd ever had about failing her filling his head.

"Footprints over here," Seth called, the sound of sirens growing louder.

Logan followed the glow of Seth's light across the narrow road and into deep foliage. Pine trees pressed in on every side, and the ground was littered with dried needles and a thin layer of new snow. He crouched near Seth's flashlight beam, studying the earth, his eyes tracking what looked to be footprints.

"He's heading up the mountain," he muttered, more to himself than to Seth.

"And he's carrying Laney. He couldn't have gotten too far." Seth moved away, silent despite his big frame.

Logan eased through the woods behind him, stepping over fallen trees as they worked their way farther up a steep incline. Seth was right. Banks would be limited to how far he could go with Laney in his arms or tossed over his shoulder.

"There's a scenic overlook a half mile from here." Logan had been there many times with Amanda and even more times after her death. The view was breathtaking, the panorama of the valley floor reminding him of the immensity of God.

He needed that reminder now.

He needed to believe that God was holding Laney's life in His hands.

"You think that's where he's heading?"

"If I wanted to dispose of a body, that's where I'd go." He

said what he was thinking because hiding the truth from Seth or from himself wouldn't help Laney.

"You lead the way then." Seth stepped to the side, and Logan jogged ahead. The trees opened up as they neared the thirty-foot cliff.

A branch cracked to the left, and he froze, his heart jumping. It could be a deer or an elk. There were plenty of them in the woods, but the hair on his arms stood on end, his body going still and taut as another branch cracked.

He tensed, staring hard into the darkness.

A shadow weaved through the trees, heading down the mountain. One person. Not two. Tall and muscular. A man. Not a woman. Banks?

It had to be.

Logan stayed hidden by trees as he stalked the figure. Another few feet and he'd be close enough to lunge. Another foot.

Now!

He threw himself forward, slamming into a solid mass, the soft huff of someone's breath spilling out and filling the air. A fist cuffed his jaw, the contact barely enough to register.

"Cool it!" He grabbed his opponent's arm, dragging it up and back.

"Get off!" Banks bucked hard.

"Where's Laney?"

"I don't know what you're talking about."

"Where is she?" Logan upped the pressure on Banks's arms, and the guy bucked again. "Keep moving, and your arm will snap."

"Snap my arm, and that'll be just one more charge added to the list of the ones stacked against you," Banks bit out.

"Where is she?"

Banks didn't respond, but he didn't move either. Obviously, the pressure on his arm was enough to keep him still. It didn't seem to be enough to get him talking, though.

Stalemate, and Laney was somewhere out in the snow.

"Leave him. We have better things to do with our time, and if we don't get to doing it, we'll be sitting in the back of a police cruiser instead of looking for Laney," Seth said.

"Let's take him along." Logan dragged Banks to his feet, keeping the attorney's arm at an angle designed for maximum pain.

A dog howled, the sound chilling.

K-9 unit already on the scent.

The cavalry rushing to the rescue.

Too bad it was probably rushing to save Banks.

A dog's howl pulled Laney from blackness into the frigid gray night. She blinked snowflakes from her lashes, her breath a white cloud in the darkness. Cold seeped through her coat and jeans and bored its way into her bones.

She had to move or she'd freeze.

She pushed against pine needles and snow, her body protesting as she sat. Trees. Everywhere. She stood on wobbly legs, her heart beating erratically. Her neck throbbed, and she pressed her hand to it. Raised welts and hot skin.

Chris!

Had he used a TASER on her?

Was he still around?

She took a step, pain shooting through her head and down her neck, something wet and warm dripping into the collar of her coat. She touched it, then brought her hands away coated with slick blood. Had she hit her head when she'd fallen? Or had Chris knocked her out?

She couldn't remember and didn't think that it mattered. Not as much as getting…

Where?

She turned in a circle.

Trees. Trees. More trees.

She felt dizzy from them.

The dog howled again, and a man called out, the voice distant but clear.

"Hello!" She tried to shout above the throb of her pulse, but her voice seemed swallowed up by the trees and the sky and the snow.

She took a step, her body swaying, a wave of nausea stealing her breath. She doubled over, wanted to sit and close her eyes. Rest against a tree trunk for just a few minutes.

Move! Her sluggish brain commanded.

She took another step, her ankle twisting as her foot landed on something hard and smooth. She tumbled forward, her balance gone, blood still oozing down the back of her neck. She lay where she'd fallen, pine needles beneath her cheek and under her hand, snow falling harder. If she lay there long enough, she'd be covered with it. A warm blanket against the chill.

Get up! It was Logan's voice this time, commanding and insistent, and she scrambled to her feet again, nearly slipping on whatever had tripped her the first time. She lifted it, fingering the smooth squarish box.

The TASER.

She clutched it in her fist as she stumbled forward, following the sound of voices, her stomach heaving, pain a white hot light behind her eyes.

Just keep moving forward, Laney. You're almost there.

William this time, his voice echoing from the past.

She stumbled, her stomach twisting.

She couldn't go another step.

Not one.

A dog barked, the sound so close she would have screamed if she could have, but there was nothing but emptiness inside. No fear. No pain. She knelt on cold wet ground, one hand against a tree trunk, the other clutching the TASER.

Get up!

She didn't know the voice, but she had to listen. Had to try. She dropped the device into her coat pocket and used both hands to push against the tree. Upright again, voices swirling in her head. Past? Present? Dream?

The dog howled, bursting through the trees in front of her, floppy ears slapping at the ground.

Real?

She reached down to touch its velvety nose, warm fur vibrating beneath her hand.

"Laney Jefferson?" A woman appeared in front of her. Laney wanted to speak, but the words seemed lost in the recesses of her mind.

"I'm Officer Danielle Sharo." The woman knelt beside her, opened a backpack and pulled a blanket out.

Laney closed her eyes. She opened them again and was lying on the ground, the blanket over her, the dog sitting nearby.

"Laney?" Logan touched her cheek, his fingers grazing over chilled skin, his warmth sinking down deep.

"I'm okay," she managed to say because the worry and grief in his eyes tugged at her heart and made her want to reassure him.

"You'd better be. I don't know what I'd do without you," he said, the words tickling the fine hair near her ears, something clinking as he moved. Cold metal brushed her cheek.

Handcuffs?

She touched his wrist.

"Are we back where we started?" she asked because she wasn't sure if they'd gone back to William's mountain cabin or if they'd ever actually left it. Maybe they'd never escaped the mountain.

"Not quite." His lips grazed hers, his tenderness filling

up every bit of emptiness in her heart, and she was helpless to stop it.

This was Logan.

Her past.

Her present.

She could let him be her future if she were brave enough.

She wanted desperately to be.

She wanted to hand over every piece of herself, give him the tiny sliver of heart that no one else had ever owned.

"I—"

"Why is he near my client? He should be in the back of a police cruiser with his buddies." Chris appeared behind Logan, his hair slicked down by snow and moisture, his bathrobe hanging open, his hands cuffed.

Good.

They were getting it right this time.

Laney wanted to close her eyes. Wanted to just sink back into the blackness, but something in Chris's eyes kept her grounded in the moment.

"We'll get this all straightened out down at the station, Chris. For now, how about you just chill?" Officer Parsons put a hand on Chris's shoulder, and Laney tried to tell him to be careful. The words stuck in her throat, carried away by the awful dizziness and pain.

"Look what he did to her!" Chris demanded.

"He didn't—" she tried to say, but he edged in closer, his face tight with rage, his voice drowning hers out.

"She's not even in her right mind. If she were, she'd be screaming."

Could Chris really be so arrogant? So sure that he'd be believed that he'd lie right in front of her?

"We've got transport on the way, Tanner. If you want to take the prisoners in, that'll be fine." Officer Sharo checked Laney's pulse and frowned.

"That's a good idea. I suggest that you take it." Chris edged even closer to Officer Sharo, his eyes blazing with the same fevered light Laney had seen before he'd TASERed her.

"Watch ou—"

Christopher knocked the officer sideways and dragged her gun from its holster. She scrambled forward, but he swung the gun toward her, toward Tanner, then pressed it against Logan's temple.

"One move, and he's dead," he said.

He was dead anyway, Laney thought. If someone didn't do something.

If *she* didn't.

She reached into her coat pocket and pulled out the TASER. Shifted.

Tanner shifted, too, his hand dropping to his service revolver.

"Don't do it, Tanner. I'd hate to have your blood on the ground, too," Chris said and the gun swung away from Logan.

Logan's gaze dropped to Laney.

"No!" he mouthed, but she was already moving, her body leaden and uncoordinated as she threw herself toward Christopher.

TWENTY-THREE

The gun exploded, the sound reverberating through the forest and through Logan. He fell back, Banks falling with him. Metal clanged against metal. He shoved at Banks's dead weight. He didn't know if the guy had been shot, he didn't care. He just had to get to Laney and make sure she was okay.

She lay crumpled on the ground. Still as death, blood seeping from the back of her head, staining the white snow.

"Laney?" He touched her cheek, his heart shuddering with fear.

"I'm okay. I think I just hit my head on something earlier," she responded but didn't open her eyes.

"That was too close," Tanner said, keys jingling as he unlocked the cuffs on Logan's wrists.

"You should have had your officer take Banks to the cruiser with Seth," Logan snapped, his voice thick, his hand shaking as he felt for Laney's pulse. She'd said she was okay, but the blood spilling onto the ground said differently.

"I wanted to give him the opportunity to show his true colors. He wouldn't have gotten that sitting in my cruiser." Tanner nudged Banks with his foot. "What'd she do to him?"

"I don't know." He just knew that if Laney died, he'd never forgive himself.

"TASER. I dropped it." Laney's eyes opened, her face colorless.

"It's here. Sorry about the gun, Tanner. I thought Randal was our biggest threat." Officer Sharo handed the TASER to Tanner.

"Lesson learned, and you'd better keep it in mind, rookie. Get the prisoner up on his feet and get him down to the patrol car." Tanner crouched on the other side of Laney, his gaze on Logan. "I knew you were innocent from the very beginning, and I've been trying to prove it for eight months."

"You think you have the proof now?"

"Danvers started singing like a jaybird about three minutes after we showed him those emails your friend sent and photocopies of his bank statement. Ten thousand dollars deposited in Danvers's account the same day as he had those meetings didn't look good. Danvers knew it. He's willing to throw Banks under the bus if it means a lighter sentence."

"So Logan is free?" Laney's words slurred, her eyes drifting closed.

"We still have some investigating to do, but I think there's a good chance all the charges will be dropped and the conviction overturned. That may still mean time in prison, you know that, right, Logan? As much as I want to skirt the law for you—"

"I know how things work, and I'm not going to fight it." Logan lifted Laney's hand and kissed her knuckles.

"We already have things in motion. We started the process as soon as we had Danvers's written confession. They've been after you for years. The way he tells it, Mildred Mackey has been gunning for you since the day she got out of prison."

"I'm sorry, Logan. It seems as if all my family has ever brought you is trouble." Laney's voice broke and a tear slipped down her cheek.

"They brought me to you. That makes it all worthwhile." He kissed her tenderly and felt her smile against his lips.

"Will you still be saying that a year from now?" she asked, her hand sliding into his, their fingers twining as EMTs moved toward them.

"Do you want me to be?" he whispered, and she looked into his eyes, looked deep and hard as if every dream she'd ever reached for might be hidden in the depth of his gaze.

"I want you to be saying it every day for the rest of our lives," she said, her hand sliding up his arm, then cupping the back of his neck, the connection between them as strong and real as any Logan had ever felt.

"I'm glad," he said, "because that's exactly what I plan to do."

EPILOGUE

"One more coat, I think," Stan said over the sound of buzz saws and hammers.

Laney stood back, eyed the whitewashed porch and nodded. "I agree."

"That's the thing that I like about you, kid. You're always agreeable. *And* you've given me a pretty nice place to stay." He grinned, his face shaded by a sun hat and his arms tan from spending a week painting the exterior of the house.

"The house is too big for just me. Besides, you make a killer lasagna." She dipped her brush into the paint can and smoothed it over the railing that her great-great grandfather had fashioned. They'd start on the back porch once the contractors were finished there, but for now, she was happy with what she saw. Happy with the life she was bringing back to the Mackey house.

"It won't be just you for long. We're five days out from the wedding. You may want me to move back to Seattle once you and your guy get back from the honeymoon." Stan smiled again, but Laney heard the question in his voice. Like her, he longed for family. He and his wife had never had children, and with Mildred back in jail, he had no one to go home to in Seattle.

But then, Seattle couldn't be his home. Not with his family in Green Bluff.

"Don't be silly. Who's going to watch the kids when I'm out with clients if you're not here? Who's going to teach them to fish and play chess while Logan is out chasing bad guys?"

"There are going to be kids?"

"Of course, and you'll be Grandpa Stan." She slung her arm around his shoulder and pretended she didn't see the tears in his eyes.

"Hey, now! You're not moving in on my wife-to-be, are you, Stan?" Logan rounded the corner of the house, and Laney's heart reached for him before her arms did. He looked so good. So strong and sturdy and trustworthy in his uniform, and he was so happy to be wearing it again. It had been three weeks since he'd finally been cleared to return to the force, and he glowed with the joy of it.

"If I were a couple of decades younger, I'd think about it, but seeing as how I'm an old man, I guess you have nothing to worry about. Now, if you two will excuse me, I need to go check on those contractors. Make sure they're not slacking. We need this place shipshape by Saturday." Stan hurried away, and Logan smiled into Laney's eyes, then pulled her into his arms.

"I missed you," he whispered as he trailed kisses up her neck.

"You saw me at church last night."

"And I haven't seen you since."

"We talked on the phone this morning." She wrapped her arms around his waist, melting into the embrace.

"I still missed you." His lips found hers. "I can't wait until Saturday, you know that?"

"Me neither."

"And you're sure that you don't mind the entire town coming to our wedding?"

"I think it's fitting. It's like we've all come full circle together."

"The church will be bursting at the seams and the gossips probably won't stop discussing the nuptials and everything that led up to them for decades," he murmured, his fingers threading through her hair.

"Let them talk," she responded, pulling him down for another kiss.

"The house looks good."

"It'll look better on Saturday. The caterer is going to set everything up in the backyard, and the church ladies insisted on bringing extra food. The reception will probably go on half the night."

"And when it's over, I'll have you all to myself." Logan grinned, and Laney's heart swelled with joy and longing.

"I'm only sorry it can't be for longer." Three days was all the time they had before Chris's trial. Laney and Logan were both testifying.

"Me, too, but we'll be coming home to this, Laney. Coming home to *us*. That's a pretty powerful thing." He tucked a strand of hair behind her ear and tenderly kissed her again.

And she knew that he alone held that little piece of heart, the one that she'd always kept so carefully to herself.

He held it gently, reverently.

He held it as if it were the only thing that he'd ever wanted.

God's plan.

She knew it was. Knew it had always been.

Nothing by chance. Everything by design. All the years together and apart finally leading them to this place called family.

* * * * *

Dear Reader,

In the darkest hours of our lives, in the times when we can't see beyond the pain of the moment, it is easy to question God's purpose and plan. Psalm 55:22 assures us that we can cast our cares on Him and that He will sustain us. That is a verse that Laney Jefferson must hold on to when her childhood friend suddenly reenters her life. Logan Randal was her defender and protector when she was a kid, but Laney isn't a kid any longer. A widow who has lived through more than her share of heartache, Laney's been struggling to hold on to her faith and to protect her broken heart. But Logan needs her help more than she needs to be safe. What begins as an effort to repay a friend turns into a struggle for survival, and Laney must learn to trust in God's promises and to believe in the power of love and second chances.

I hope you enjoy reading Laney and Logan's story, and I pray that, through the good and bad times, you will know the truth of God's love for you.

Blessings,

Shirlee McCoy

Questions for Discussion

1. Logan Randal has been through plenty of difficult times in his life. Where does he find the strength to keep fighting for what he knows is right?

2. Laney Jefferson ran from a difficult childhood and created a good life out of the ashes of something horrible. What did she learn from her troubles? How does it affect the way she views the world?

3. Describe the bond that ties Laney and Logan. How is it different from or the same as the bond Laney had with her husband?

4. Do you think there can only be one great love in a person's life, or is it possible to find love more than once? Explain.

5. How did losing her husband change Laney's heart toward God?

6. Logan is running for his freedom and his life. Even in the midst of his trials, he knows that God is in control. Have you been through great difficulties in your life? How did it affect your faith and your relationship with God?

7. Laney lived a lie during her childhood, covering up her parents' abuse. How does that shape her values and beliefs as an adult?

8. How does her relationship with her parents shape her relationship with God?

9. Laney feels that she owes Logan for the help he gave her when she was a child. Is that the only reason why she helps him? Explain your view on this.

10. Would you ever help a fugitive? Why or why not?

11. Logan remembers Laney as a scared young girl. Seeing her years later, he discovers that she's grown into a strong and capable woman. What is it about Laney that appeals to him?

12. Laney isn't looking for a second chance at love. Her heart was broken when her husband died, and she's not willing to risk it again. Have you ever had your heart broken? How difficult was it to open up again?

13. Even in the darkest times, God is with us, offering refuge and help during our times of need. Describe a time in your life when you have cried out to God and found comfort and help in Him.

REQUEST YOUR FREE BOOKS!

2 FREE RIVETING INSPIRATIONAL NOVELS
PLUS 2 FREE MYSTERY GIFTS

Love Inspired®
SUSPENSE

YES! Please send me 2 FREE Love Inspired® Suspense novels and my 2 FREE mystery gifts (gifts are worth about $10). After receiving them, if I don't wish to receive any more books, I can return the shipping statement marked "cancel." If I don't cancel, I will receive 4 brand-new novels every month and be billed just $4.74 per book in the U.S. or $5.24 per book in Canada. That's a savings of at least 21% off the cover price. It's quite a bargain! Shipping and handling is just 50¢ per book in the U.S. and 75¢ per book in Canada.* I understand that accepting the 2 free books and gifts places me under no obligation to buy anything. I can always return a shipment and cancel at any time. Even if I never buy another book, the two free books and gifts are mine to keep forever.

123/323 IDN F5AC

Name _____ (PLEASE PRINT) _____

Address _____ Apt. # _____

City _____ State/Prov. _____ Zip/Postal Code _____

Signature (if under 18, a parent or guardian must sign)

Mail to the Harlequin® Reader Service:
IN U.S.A.: P.O. Box 1867, Buffalo, NY 14240-1867
IN CANADA: P.O. Box 609, Fort Erie, Ontario L2A 5X3

**Are you a current subscriber to Love Inspired Suspense books
and want to receive the larger-print edition?
Call 1-800-873-8635 or visit www.ReaderService.com.**

* Terms and prices subject to change without notice. Prices do not include applicable taxes. Sales tax applicable in N.Y. Canadian residents will be charged applicable taxes. Offer not valid in Quebec. This offer is limited to one order per household. Not valid for current subscribers to Love Inspired Suspense books. All orders subject to credit approval. Credit or debit balances in a customer's account(s) may be offset by any other outstanding balance owed by or to the customer. Please allow 4 to 6 weeks for delivery. Offer available while quantities last.

Your Privacy—The Harlequin® Reader Service is committed to protecting your privacy. Our Privacy Policy is available online at www.ReaderService.com or upon request from the Harlequin Reader Service.
We make a portion of our mailing list available to reputable third parties that offer products we believe may interest you. If you prefer that we not exchange your name with third parties, or if you wish to clarify or modify your communication preferences, please visit us at www.ReaderService.com/consumerschoice or write to us at Harlequin Reader Service Preference Service, P.O. Box 9062, Buffalo, NY 14269. Include your complete name and address.

LIS13R

SPECIAL EXCERPT FROM

Love Inspired.
SUSPENSE

Crime is escalating in Sagebrush, Texas, and Texas K-9 Unit trainer Kaitlin Mathers is the crime syndicate's next target.

Read on for a preview of the exciting conclusion to the Texas K-9 Unit series, LONE STAR PROTECTOR by Lenora Worth, available June 2013.

"Don't make a sound."

K-9 trainer Kaitlin Mathers felt the cold muzzle of the gun sticking into her rib cage. The man holding her wore black coveralls and a black ski mask. She had to keep her head so she wouldn't be killed. So she could get away.

Across the K-9 training yard, Warrior barked and snarled from his mesh kennel porch. Thankfully, she hadn't put the young trainee inside for the night yet. Someone would hear the barking and come around the corner, wouldn't they?

It had never occurred to Kaitlin that anyone would be hiding right outside the doors of the Sagebrush K-9 Training Facility. Especially since the building and training yard were directly behind the Sagebrush Police Headquarters.

The man holding her must have known the risks, but he'd somehow managed to get through that gate. He hurriedly shoved her toward a waiting van.

Kaitlin looked at the van, then tried to look back at her attacker. Before she could see anything, he jerked her back around and pushed the gun hard against her side. "Let's go."

If she got into that van, the chances were very good that she'd be dead by nightfall. She screamed.

K-9 Captain Slade McNeal was halfway to his vehicle when he heard barking. Excited barking. Whirling toward the kennels, he wondered which dog had been left.

Warrior.

He'd just watched Kaitlin Mathers putting the newbie through his paces. They'd spoken briefly, and he'd gone back to his office.

But where was Kaitlin now? It wasn't like her to leave a dog unattended.

Slade hurried toward the building, his weapon drawn. He passed the kennels, but didn't see anyone.

Then he heard a scream.

Slade stood at the corner of the building and pivoted around the side, his weapon still drawn. A man in a dark mask was trying to drag Kaitlin toward a black van. And he had a gun pointed at her head.

He recognized this man. The Ski-Mask Man. Slade had been gunning for him for five long months. Could this case finally get a break?

"Drop the weapon," Slade shouted. "Now!"

For the heart-stopping conclusion to the
Texas K-9 Unit series, pick up
LONE STAR PROTECTOR by Lenora Worth,
available June 2013 from Love Inspired Suspense.

Love Inspired®
SUSPENSE
RIVETING INSPIRATIONAL ROMANCE

RUNNING OUT OF TIME...

After two months of protective custody, bodyguard Arianna Jackson is days away from testifying at a murder trial when the unthinkable happens. Her Alaska safe house is attacked, and Arianna is forced to go on the run with U.S. Marshal Brody Callahan. Arianna is used to issuing orders, not taking them, but now, out in the wild, with a bounty on her head and a killer on her heels, she has only one hope of making it to testify—the handsome protector at her side.

GUARDIANS, INC.

GUARDING THE WITNESS
by
MARGARET DALEY

Available June 2013 wherever books are sold.

www.LoveInspiredBooks.com

LIS44541

Love Is Only A Letter Away

So what if Joann Yoder's Amish community deems her a spinster? She's content to stay single. In the meantime, she's working hard to finally buy her dream house. So it's problematic when she's fired from her job to make room for the owner's nephew, Roman Weaver. His blue eyes aside, she simply can't stand him! Good thing she has the secret letters she's been exchanging with a mystery man to keep her going. But who is the man writing her letters? And could she possibly fall for him in real life, too?

BRIDES OF
Amish Country

Plain Admirer

by

Patricia Davids

Available June 2013

www.LoveInspiredBooks.com

LI0513